A Zaria Fierce Novel

# Christoffer Johansen and the Return to Jötunheim

## Written and Illustrated by
## Keira Gillett

E-book ISBN: 978-1-942750-13-0

Paperback ISBN: 978-1-942750-14-7

LCCN: 2020905566

Snatch book two for FREE
Sign up for Keira Gillett's newsletter

**Special Offer:** You can snatch book two for free when you sign up for Keira Gillett's mailing list. Grab your copy of *Zaria Fierce and the Enchanted Drakeland Sword* in the e-book format of your choice.

**Join Team Fierce Today:**

# Reading Order:

# Praise for Zaria Fierce and the Secret of Gloomwood Forest

"Are you in the mood for an old fashioned magical jaunt? Zaria Fierce and the Secret of Gloomwood Forest by Keira Gillett is a classic "perilous adventure" book for middle grade readers." *Jennifer Bardsley, The YA Gal*

"A captivating blending of fantasy storytelling with today's technology. At the base of this tale is deep, abiding friendship that stands the tests of time, adventure and even danger." *Kathy Haw, Goodreads Review*

"If you're looking for an action-packed adventure dipped in fantasy, look no further. This book kept me on my toes with its many cliffhangers and plot twists; it was quite hard to put down at times." *Meredith, All 'Bout Them Books and Stuff*

"This was a really good book with a great setting and cool plot line. I really liked how it didn't hide that Zaria was adopted and she knew it. I also liked how her adoptive parents were nice. You don't see that often in books (as an adopted kid, I like it when adoption is portrayed well)." *Erik, This Kid Reviews Books*

"A great book with vivid descriptions and relatable characters. The main character becomes a strong female lead, and the writing and illustrations make this fantasy world even more real and interesting." *Analee, Book Snacks*

# Praise for Zaria Fierce and the Enchanted Drakeland Sword

"The Zaria Fierce series just keeps getting better, with this sequel! This is an awesome fantasy filled with suspense, from the first page to the last! The vivid descriptions combined with the beautiful illustrations make the setting come to life." *Brandi Nyborg, Goodreads Review*

"This is one of the most amazing second books in a trilogy that I've read. I like how empowering the book is, especially on facing your own demons. Just like Zaria." *Danissa, The Booklandia*

"I like how the action begins quickly and Gillett brings the reader up to speed on the plot, no time is wasted in getting these friends off on another adventure through the Norwegian countryside. Oh, and that setting, it's one of the most enjoyable things in reading Gillett's stories. All the lovely rich details of each of the magical kingdoms, each place is unique and highlights the depth of her imagination." *Brenda, Log Cabin Library*

"Zaria is both vulnerable and strong, and very much a role model for my own daughters." *APinFL, Audible Review*

# Praise for Zaria Fierce and the Dragon Keeper's Golden Shoes

"The Zaria Fierce trilogy is a fun middle grade adventure with a great message, and *Zaria Fierce and the Dragon Keeper's Golden Shoes* rounds it out perfectly! Zaria and her friends are realistic characters and I thoroughly appreciated the exploration of their friendship and growth as individuals and as a group. I think the Zaria Fierce series deserves a lot more love!" *Nicole, Read Eat Sleep Repeat*

"*Zaria Fierce and the Dragon Keeper's Golden Shoes* was the magical conclusion this trilogy asked for. Filled with action and adventure, Zaria and her friends showed us the importance of teamwork, friendship, and having courage in ourselves. The perfect ending to a fun series, I recommend this to all fantasy lovers, middle school and beyond!" *Emily, Midwestern Book Nerd*

"*Zaria Fierce and the Dragon Keeper's Golden Shoes* was a spectacular conclusion to a great trilogy (though the ending left the door open for more adventures). Filled with magic, a great story line, amazing and real characters, wonderful settings and beautifully explored themes, Keira Gillett created a trilogy that I will always cherish and will visit anytime. If you like The Chronicles of Narnia, *The Hobbit,* The Spiderwick Chronicles or simply love a book filled with Norwegian folklore and fantasy, then this is the ultimate series for you to read, devour and lose yourselves in." *Ner, A Cup of Coffee and a Book*

# Praise for Aleks Mickelsen and the Twice-Lost Fairy Well

"You don't realise how much you miss things till they are gone, and this is the case with this series. The characters had a way of worming themselves into my heart and I missed them! Well, they are back and better than ever!!" *Natalie, Book Lover's Life*

"I loved the first three Zaria books and I have to say I'm even more in love with Aleks! I was surprised by the many twists and turns of the book and loved catching up with all the new and old characters. This book would be a great gift for any young teenager and it's a great read for an adult like myself." *Rusty Forsmark, Amazon Review*

"There is so much that I loved about this story. Aleks is one of my favorite characters and I am so excited that he is getting his own stories so that readers can learn more about him and go on this journey of self-discovery along with him and his friends." *Bridgett, Little Bee's Reads*

"I must find a way to sneak a stargazer along with a thousand pesky request letters in the mail to the author to try to get the next book to come out faster!" *Ronald Shaw, Audible Review*

# Praise for Aleks Mickelsen and the Call of the White Raven

"This volume of the Zaria Fierce series feels like a fun camping trip. A combination of an adventure and a love story. Entertaining from beginning to end and recommended." *Christian, Audible Review*

"Everything you love about the Zaria Fierce books is here: the strong friendships, the nonstop adventure, the magical creatures, and the hero's quest are all here, waiting for fantasy lovers to join them. Keira Gillett's at the height of her storytelling here;" *Rosemary, Mom Read It*

"I really enjoyed this next book. Aleks is definitely becoming my favorite character in the series. Seeing him face his fear, and his fate, in accepting who he is, has made me think, and reminds me of my own individual quest for identity." *Daniel, Audible Review*

# Praise for Aleks Mickelsen and the Eighth Fox Throne War

"From the opening sentence of the prologue to the final paragraph, you know you are in a fierce adventure. Having been with the series since the beginning, it has been wonderful following our group through all the action! *Aleks Mickelsen and the Eighth Fox Throne War* abounds with magic and if fey politics don't get you killed, the dragon just might ... or a beautiful fairy's father... Settle in and get ready for a great story from one of my favorite authors." *Tammy Spencer, Goodreads Review*

"I held my breath many times reading this book. The challenges are nonstop. You'll find plenty of fierce battles and extremely scary creatures. But, as always in this series, friendship, cooperation, and just the right amount of humor offer hope in the darkest of times." *Patricia Mather Parker, Author of The Abode*

"Keira does it again in the third Aleks Mickelsen book! Full of adventure, the story continues on as the gang tries to fool the plans of Fritjof, a dragon that is sneakier than a snake. Keira's writing always impresses me... A highly enjoyable read for all ages!" *Amanda, Goodreads Review*

## Dedication:

This book is dedicated to some amazing people who let me pick their brains – Tommy, Lizzy, Nate, Tammy, Nicole, Matt, and Morten. Thanks for the help!

## To Readers:

Christoffer is one of my favorite characters in this series. He brings laughter and light to those around him. What's not to love? Okay, maybe some of his jokes, but you have to start building your set somewhere, right? Ultimately, what made me want to tell his tale is that he's heroic, but doesn't think of himself as a hero. I really wanted to tackle that idea. I don't know about you, but I think it's a good lesson for us to internalize that a hero can be anyone, anywhere, and that sometimes the bravest things anyone can do are to be kind and to be yourself.

# Table of Contents

# Prologue: The Unlikely Hero

Christoffer Johansen loved magic and adventure, and not just the Dungeon and Dragons variety. Dragons even featured heavily in his previous adventures with his friends. Fighting dragons and monsters within the confines of a game was, all said and done, an excellent way to pass the time. Fighting dragons in real life, not so much. It got scary, scaly, and lethal real fast, and he didn't have his character's sorcerer powers to protect him in the real world, which wasn't to say he was without powerful friends of the magical variety. Magic was indeed very, very real.

As if pulled straight out of the fictional and fantasy worlds he loved, wide-area-effect spells and enchanted dragon-defying swords belonged to his best friend Zaria Fierce. With dark brown braided hair, eyes a purple so electric they practically glowed in the dark, and the ability to turn out a feast on short notice, she was the epitome of a true sorceress and dragon slayer. He only played at it... and only when she wasn't around.

They say imitation is the sincerest form of flattery, but he'd be mortified if she ever found out about Fredrick the Festivus and his talking sword Flayzor. Not that her sword ever talked. In fact, the Drakeland Sword – the only sword to ever slay a dragon – lay broken in a dozen shards, carefully wrapped and hidden in the back of her closet.

Zaria hadn't yet told Queen Helena of the Under Realm, her birth mother, what had happened to it during the battle between Fritjof, the youngest of the three original dragon brothers, and Aleks, their changeling friend and recently crowned fairy king. Opting to keep its destruction a secret, she clearly hoped to avoid ever having to tell her illustrious parent the truth, but Christoffer thought that wouldn't last very long. The sword was too important an object in the war on dragons. Something would have to be done about it sooner rather than later.

His wingman and Stag Lord of the ellefolken, Henrik Woodworth, would probably persuade her to tell the powerful, ancient – yet age-defying – sorceress the truth. If the magical-friend-fights-a-dragon pattern continued, the brown-haired, blue-eyed prince would be the next to face down a formidable dragon.

Ever since Zaria took out Koll, and Aleks managed to defeat Fritjof – effectively removing two brothers from the equation – he'd been thinking about the final dragon and what would happen next. He'd never mention his theory to the others, as they would tell him not to tempt fate, but he couldn't help himself. It just made sense. One original brother remained and so, too, one extraordinary friend. The math just worked.

He just hoped the rest of that equation also held true – especially the part where the magical-friend-fights-a-dragon-and-lives-to-tell-the-tale. It would royally suck if it didn't – all applicable puns intended. It had been a pretty close call with Zaria and Aleks, what with she being eaten, and he getting sliced to ribbons. A flame-broiled Henrik would be unlikely to end well.

Christoffer didn't hold out that he was an unlikely hero. He knew who he was – a loveable sidekick. In real life, not D&D. In D&D he was a powerful force for good, even if his sword was more chaotic-neutral. In the real world, his status as sidekick was well established, and that's all he'd ever be. How could he be anything else with his goofy sense of humor, and his ability to wax poetic on the finer points of were-bear grooming? He'd resigned himself to the role good naturedly. After all, there wasn't much else he could do with magical friends like the ones he had, other than to accept his loyal sidekick status and provide the best support he could.

Christoffer took comfort that he wasn't the only human in the group, and the fact that if he couldn't have powers, at least his best friends did. Sometimes it was about who one knew and what they knew and could do. He'd much rather know about magic than be left in the dark. It brought to mind a joke.

A sorceress princess, a fairy king, and an ellefolken prince all walk into a bar... and make friends with a bunch of humans.

Standing amongst the regular homo sapien ranks were his good friends Geirr Engelstad and Filip Storstrand. Geirr liked to fly planes, and had recently been cleared of fault after an investigation into a crash that happened thirteen months ago. It was a good thing, too, because telling the authorities, "A dragon made me do it," just wasn't in the cards. Christoffer was hopeful to fly with Geirr the next time he went up. Having already secured his father's approval, all that remained was getting his mother to sign off on it (easier said than done.)

These days Filip was overwhelmingly sentimental. He and Zaria had begun dating each other as soon as they got back from Niffleheim after Fritjof's defeat. Every time he spoke about her he gushed and lost his train of thought. Their relationship only seemed to grow stronger as the days passed. The two were so sweet on each other, it could make even the biggest humbug smile, and definitely put the Stag Lord out of sorts whenever they were in each other's company for long.

All Filip wanted in life was to be her knight in shining armor, a role Christoffer knew Henrik also secretly wanted for himself. In fact, everybody knew the Stag Lord's feelings – that is everybody, but Zaria. Even Filip knew, and knowing his good fortune for what it was, did his best to win the title of World's Best Boyfriend every day.

He did all the chivalrous things – walking her to school and home again, holding doors open, and carrying her book bag (and that was truly saying something, because Zaria was a serious bookworm and seemed to lug four or five heavy volumes around at all times). "Life is full of little downtimes, that's when I get all my best reading done," she'd been known to say defensively to his teasing.

On the flip side, Zaria, in turn, did a lot of nice things for Filip. She conjured up picnic blankets and prepped all their lunches on the quad. She tutored him in history and literature, and bought him a new T-shirt for his birthday with one of his favorite characters, the Black Knight from *Monty Python and the Holy Grail,* splashed across the front.

Christoffer was extremely happy for them, even if he wished for a little romance for himself and some for his miserable princeling friend. He'd decided this year to do something about it and looked forward to where his efforts would take him. Princes needed the best wingmen, or perhaps the best wingmen were princes. He hadn't decided.

One day, someday, hopefully soon, he'd have his own turn to shine and be counted among his heroic friends. It didn't need to be facing down a dragon and emerging victorious. He didn't aim so high. He would happily settle for a date to the year's first school dance. Maybe he could get Henrik to sing his praises to that sweet little violinist in third period. Maybe she had a friend for the Stag Lord, too. Wouldn't that be something!

# Chapter One: Not Another Kidnapping!

This was no typical Tuesday. Christoffer looked forward to the evening when his younger sisters would participate in their first ballet recital. At five years old the twins were more apt to trip on their tutus than twirl in them, but the imagined sparkly, gurgling sound of their laughter and bright, innocent eyes already put a smile on his face.

Hiking the strap of his backpack higher on his shoulder, Christoffer made his way to school, enjoying the cool crisp air that wasn't quite autumn and wasn't quite winter. When he reached the scrollwork bridge, it didn't cross his mind to look for bridge trolls, and he strolled over its threshold with a sure and even step.

His best friend Zaria would be coming later, escorted by Filip. The thought of them turned his mood wistful. Christoffer wished he, too, could find someone special, but he didn't let it bother him long. He might not have found the one, but he was having fun looking. Shaking off the lingering melancholy, he turned his attention to the social dance this Friday. He hoped to coerce Henrik into joining him, so that the two of them could flirt and dance with girls from the international dance club.

This weekend they'd continue their salsa lessons at the community center, and while Christoffer enjoyed the spectacle, Henrik generally shied away. The Stag Lord needed to get over Zaria. It'd been a year, and she and Filip were stronger than ever. Soon, everyone would be graduating and matriculating to universities and if Henrik didn't shake himself out of his funk, he'd miss his chance with other equally pretty and nice girls.

Gazing about at the city around him, Christoffer zeroed in on the unwelcome sight of a tall, lanky figure standing at the far end of the bridge.

"Oh, come on now," he whined. "I don't want to be kidnapped again. I've got plans this weekend. Good plans. Great plans, even."

The river-troll cocked his head inquisitively, raising his webbed hands in supplication. "Olaf be not kidnapping you. I be asking for your help."

Suspicious, Christoffer asked, "If you need help, why are you asking me and not Zaria?"

Olaf scowled. "I be not bothering her with me troubles just yet. I be needing another pair of eyes. You be doing the job nicely."

"Gee, thanks," said Christoffer dryly. "You know, I really have to get to school, and I've got this thing after with my baby sisters. What about Queen Helena? Is she free?"

"She still be recovering from the last dragon. She not be needing more worries."

"Queen Helena's still recovering? Zaria didn't mention this," Christoffer said, concerned. "How is she watching over the dragons?"

"She not be watching. She be with me in my river, away from the wretched things," Olaf said. "Only way to heal."

"But the Under Realm," protested Christoffer. "It needs to be protected."

Olaf waved his hands. "It be protected. King Hector be guarding it."

"No offense, but Hector's a tree," scoffed Christoffer. "I get how he and the Golden Kings keep the dragons from escaping the Under Realm through the barrier of their roots, but Fritjof was able to breach them just a year ago. Who's to say another dragon can't do the same?"

"Look, boy," Olaf growled, causing the hairs to rise on the back of Christoffer's neck. "It be not for you to decide. Queen Helena be very weak, and she needing to be free of their presence for a time. Somebody need be protecting her like she always be protecting us."

"Okay, okay, fine," said Christoffer, giving in. "But I think you should tell this to Zaria. She should know how her mum's doing."

"Olaf not be asking her for help unless it be absolutely necessary. Her mother tell me she not be wanting her involved in Under Realm business until there be no other options. Come with me. I must show you this."

He canted his head. "I'm confused. Didn't you just say that Queen Helena didn't know?"

"She not be, but Queen Helena still be wanting Zaria away from the dragons. She wanting her to be a normal girl for as long as possible."

"I think that ship has sailed," said Christoffer, wryly.

"It be not for us to decide," said Olaf, waving his long-fingered hands vaguely.

Despite himself, Christoffer asked, "So, you think you found something related to dragons?"

Instead of answering, the troll half-turned and beckoned, "Come."

"Oh, all right, I'm coming," said Christoffer, shrugging his backpack high on his shoulder again. "Let's go."

He shook his head at his own folly as he accepted Olaf's outstretched hand. The cool slick feeling of scales met his warm palm in a disconcerting fashion. Christoffer tried not to grimace as he clambered on top of the wrought-iron railing.

The languid water flowed by in a constant, soft burble as it lapped against the rocky embankment. Looking down at their wavering reflections, he could not imagine he'd willingly be doing something like this, not even in a million years.

"We be jumping on three," said Olaf, twitching his long, thin fingers.

The water churned, at first sluggishly, and then faster and faster until a whirlpool frothed and foamed. The scene reminded him of another whirlpool and another time four years ago.

Back then, he'd been terrified of Olaf. The river-troll had kidnapped him for trespassing on his bridge, but never once asked for a toll. Christoffer had thought he was a goner – that nobody would know what happened to him, not even Zaria. He hadn't taken her seriously, and had convinced her sight unseen that the troll was an old, homeless vagabond.

He learned his lesson the hard way that day.

"Three!" shouted Olaf, jumping from the bridge.

Christoffer, who'd been absorbed in his thoughts, jerked out of his daydreams. He hadn't even heard numbers One and Two, and if he didn't want to be left behind, he'd have to jump. Knowing the passageway would close as soon as the troll disappeared beneath its roiling surface, he threw himself off the bridge.

He sank like a stone, plummeting straight through the freezing whirlpool. Spinning and spiraling downward, he was sucked into the heart of Olaf's watery realm, fathoms deeper than the actual river. Landing with a plop and a splash, Christoffer dripped all over the soft sandy floor, which did a fine job absorbing it.

Beyond being drenched, it wasn't all bad to be returning to the scene of the crime, as it were. The river-troll's home glimmered and glistened under the sun's filtered reflections on the waves. It was peaceful and calming, with every sound muffled and muted, like being in the heart of a sanctuary.

He looked up and could just make out the dark, hazy shape of the bridge as they floated away from it. Never stationary, Olaf's home moved with the currents – and the river-troll's whims. Right now, those whims led them away from Fredrikstad.

The troll beckoned him to follow to a sparse, casual, white and gray circular seating arrangement at the bubble's very center. The effect was inviting, not intimidating, and Christoffer wondered if it was because Queen Helena had something to do with it. He sincerely doubted that Olaf had taken up interior decorating since the last time he'd been in his home or more aptly prison – with a bedrock mattress and a fishy-smelling blanket to match.

He looked around searching for any sign of something reminiscent of his last visit. He felt a little silly examining everything because he hadn't been in this room before. Deciding to be grateful that the moist, damp feel was missing, he slouched onto one of a pair of plush, low-back chairs with a *squelch* and wiggled off his shoes, so he could bury his toes in the sandy river bottom.

Craning his neck, Christoffer didn't spy any doors or passageways to other rooms, and wondered not for the first time how Olaf moved around his realm. The last time he'd been in Olaf's home, he'd been trapped in a one-bubble room much like this one, only smaller. There hadn't been any doors then, either. Not even temporary glowing magical ones. He'd checked.

Not once when Olaf delivered him food, or came by to taunt him about his friends' progress searching for Hart, had a doorway opened. The river-troll had simply appeared in the room. The privilege and prerogative of being the sole purveyor of his domain was established in those tormenting visits.

When Olaf freed him, it wasn't like a cell had been unlocked. He hadn't walked through a door. No, it was better to describe it like being spat out a whale's blowhole. He just sort of plopped out of the bubble and onto the surface, soaked to the bone in freezing water and smelling like fish.

He hoped they wouldn't have to leave in a similar manner. Surely now that Olaf was friend and not foe, there had to be a better way to disembark than being shot from a whale's air cannon. Maybe they would exit on a gust of air and seafoam, clothes dry, with perfectly windswept hair looking perfectly noble and dashing. Or not. A guy could dream, right? He wrung out the hem of his shirt.

A platter of warm chocolate chip cookies and cold glasses of milk had been set on a table between the chairs. That looked promising. He took one and put it on a plate, bit into it, and sank back with a sigh. At least this time around there was more space, comfier furniture, and the food was better.

"Where's Queen Helena?" asked Christoffer, around a mouthful of cookie.

Olaf waved vaguely. "She be resting somewhere close by where the ellefolken tents be. She wants to be near at hand in case of danger."

"Where are you taking us?" he asked, accepting another cookie from the platter proffered him.

"I be getting us to where be the Glomma and Gjöll rivers meet."

"How soon before we get there?" asked Christoffer. "What are you going to show me?"

"You be full of questions," Olaf observed. "I not be remembering that."

He shrugged eloquently and ate another cookie. "I'm not a prisoner this time. Also, I'm not scared of being eaten by you or sold off to a dwarvish slave mine if I annoy you or break a rule."

"Hmm," hummed Olaf, noncommittedly. "It still could be arranged."

Christoffer laughed and puffed out his chest. "After all we've been through, I'm as fearless as they come. Bring it on."

"If you be saying so," replied the troll, snacking on a cookie. He ate it in two quick bites, brushed crumbs off his face, and calmly turned to his guest. "As for what Olaf be showing you, it be not easy to explain. Better be for human to see first, before you be trying to understand."

"Try me," challenged Christoffer. "I'm not some lame-brain goblin."

"Funny, you be mentioning goblins," Olaf said, heaving himself upright and out of his chair. "We be here. Follow me, and tell me what you be thinking."

"Really?" questioned Christoffer, glancing curiously through the bubble's warped and wavy surface. "That hardly took any time at all. Dare I hope I get back in time for lunch?"

"My river, my magic, my rules," said the river-troll with a satisfied gleam in his eyes. "Besides, it be almost noon already."

"You're kidding me," Christoffer exclaimed, looking at his phone. Sure enough, it was ten to noon. His battery was also seriously depleted. He turned it off.

Olaf, head canted, studied his reaction. Consolingly, he said, "You be human. Your perception of time be a little warped from the beginning. Why do you think the stargazer be working its magic on you?"

Christoffer pouted. "I can't help being human, you know."

"Aye, you be right about that," agreed Olaf, commiserating. "Glad to be a river-troll meself. I would hate to be human. Now come and look."

Christoffer decided not to tell the troll he was glad not to be him, too. That seemed unnecessary. Standing, he ambled over to Olaf near the edge of the bubble. One of the troll's bony fingers pointed straight out at a forty-five degree angle. Following its path, he squinted under the bright glare from the sun and tried to make out the dark shapes.

"What am I looking at?" he asked.

Olaf rolled his eyes. "Goblins. What else be they?"

Shading his gaze, he looked again. The dark blobs slowly coalesced into figures. The longer he stared the more details emerged as Olaf smoothed and settled the waves. A trio of goblins lingered along the embankment. Christoffer couldn't be sure if their ugly faces were from the ripples in the water or if they'd been born that way.

Black, fathomless eyes against waxy, green skin the exact shade of a rubber plant's leaves, were glazed over in ecstasy. Small, needle-thin teeth ripped callously into fish flesh. Guts and gore hung from dripping, drooling mouths. Christoffer's stomach clenched at the sight, the cookies threatening to make a reappearance.

"Filthy, disgusting creatures," muttered Olaf.

"Why are they here?" asked Christoffer.

"That be the question I would be liking answered," said the troll, darkly. "None be daring enough to come to my water's edge before, and I not be able to scare them off. They be laughing at me when I try, and these not be the only ones."

Christoffer stared at him and wiggled his fingers. "Not even with your river magic?"

Olaf shook his head. "They be protected somehow. They be not fearing me. Someone has their allegiance I be certain of it."

"That's bad," he said, finally understanding Olaf's concern. "That's, like, really bad. We should tell Zaria and Queen Helena."

"Perhaps," agreed Olaf. "First, however, you be trying to scare them off."

"Me?" asked Christoffer, incredulous. "Why me?"

"Because goblins fear humans more than any others that be walking on the earth, except for maybe ghouls."

Watching them savage their meal, Christoffer couldn't believe it. "Why?"

"Vikings considered them vermin, and made it a great sport to hunt them down with dogs."

"I didn't bring Defender with me. It's just me," Christoffer pointed out.

"You carry the smell of a dog," said Olaf. "It be worth the attempt. We be needing to get you downwind so they be smelling you."

Christoffer raised his arm and sniffed at a dry spot on his shirt. It smelled like laundry detergent to him. He didn't get dog at all. Curiously, he tried his jeans, sniffing at the knee. Not as fresh as his shirt, but definitely not funky. Skeptical, he nonetheless agreed and donned his damp shoes.

Olaf showed him that there was, indeed, a second method of leaving the bubble room – one preferable to his first experience. The two emerged from the bubble by walking up and over, and down and out of a reflective ledge, a glimmering edge between the watery realm and the air and earth outside of it. It felt like moving between levels on M.C. Escher lithographs, stunning, but impossible... and yet... somehow foot and mind worked to make it happen.

In the forest, the crunching, munching sounds set Christoffer's teeth on edge. Disgust gripped him by the throat, and he did all he could to keep from gagging at the auditory assault. Olaf dragged him through the trees, dashing up and around fallen branches and rough stones. It wasn't hard to keep up and Christoffer felt as nimble as an elf. They quickly reached the top of an overlook directly across from the oblivious goblins.

"Scare them," Olaf reminded him unnecessarily, before jumping down and scurrying off.

"How?" he asked; but, the troll was gone.

Stooping to pick up some loose rocks, he stood and took careful aim. Hurling the first rock, Christoffer watched it sail and clack satisfyingly above their heads. As one, they stopped eating and looked toward the source of the sound, starring dumbly at the trees around them.

The next stone bounced off a tree trunk and smacked into the back of the largest one's head. It snarled, twisting and turning on the spot. A strong breeze blew past Christoffer and the trio froze in place before their gazes tracked his location.

Christoffer waved. "Hello goblins, fancy seeing you here at Chef Olaf's Table. It's time to pay your tab; the restaurant is closing."

The largest, gnarliest one hissed, saliva and something else – which Christoffer refused to identify – dripping from its needle-sharp teeth. "Human."

The other two squealed and squawked, repeating dumbly, "Human. Human."

"Not exactly the response I was hoping for, there," said Christoffer, wondering if the two were as dumb as they appeared. "Should I sic my dog on you?"

He made a lunging move toward them and the goblins all scrambled back, dropping their meals in their haste. Confident that they would flee, Christoffer lurched forward again. The leader stumbled back another step, one hand barely grasping the remains of his fish. Its gaze frantically searched behind him for the dog that wouldn't be coming.

"Go on, get out of here!" he shouted, taking a running step.

The weaker two raced back toward the trees, but the leader, undeterred, sniffed, then sneered, "No dog."

"No dog?" the two questioned nervously.

"Uh oh," said Christoffer, shifting his weight, preparing for a fight or flight response.

The leader's eyes narrowed as it sniffed the air again. "No dog," he confirmed. "Only human."

The other two cried, "Human. Human."

"Argh!" Christoffer bellowed, flapping his arms, trying to scare them off, but the goblins stayed firm and shifted their stances, poised to fight. Their greedy eyes devoured him from afar.

"Eat human," said the leader.

"Eat. Eat," the others parroted.

"Argh! Mistake!" Christoffer cried, turning quickly as the three lunged at him with wide, salivating mouths.

"Over here," shouted Olaf, appearing just ahead.

Following, he ran back up the rocks and down the other side. Stumbling over loose gravel, he kicked out at grasping, greedy fingers. The goblin yelped in pain, but the leader dragged it forward and shoved it back toward Christoffer, where it snapped at him like a rabid animal.

The other one got underfoot, tripping him and sending him sprawling. They were so close he could feel their hot breaths on his neck. He gulped, elbowing and kicking out again, managing to knock one down, as Olaf gripped his outstretched forearm and hauled him upright.

"They don't scare easily," panted Christoffer, staring at Olaf as the troll's narrowed yellow gaze glanced behind them, while a fresh wave of garbled insults frothed from the leader toward the whining, wounded goblin clutching its nose.

"Or they be not scared of you," said Olaf, grumpily, angling for the river. "If I waited for the Stag Lord, might be a different story."

"He *is* ripped. Definitely a much more physically intimidating fellow than I am. The witch sure does like making him work out. I wonder what that's all about." He waggled his eyebrows.

Olaf grunted. "We must be hurrying, while they be distracted. Try to avoid being bitten by one of them."

"I don't fancy getting my leg shredded," he agreed, leaping over a log. The sight of Christoffer and Olaf getting away forced the arguing trio into action, and they tore after them.

"It be venomous – their bite," the river-troll corrected, his breathing heavy. "You be paralyzed."

Passing by a large tree branch, Christoffer grabbed it and turned around swinging. He whacked the leader in the face, sending him sprawling. The other two hesitated and whimpered, cowering. Their leader snarled and swiped at them, irritated, forcing them to dance back.

"We be almost there," huffed Olaf.

Christoffer dropped the branch and turned away from the goblins, following after the troll's lanky form. In the background he heard the leader rouse the other two and start the chase again, but they were too late to catch their prey. One second Christoffer and Olaf were running side by side and the next the river-troll took a flying leap through the air. He plunged into the water, and disappeared.

"Bombs away!" whooped Christoffer, taking a running leap and following Olaf into the swirling vortex of the Glomma.

# Chapter Two: The Queen's Quest

"What's next?" asked Christoffer with a grin, elated at their daring escape.

The sandy floor beneath his feet turned muddy from the influx of water. He walked forward, ignoring the way the sand sucked at his shoes and water ran down the backs of his legs to pool in his socks. The damp siphoned the warmth from his skin, causing him to shiver, and he chaffed his arms.

Wringing out his clothes, his earlier elation evaporated. With a rueful grimace he wished Madam Brown were around. If she were, she could dry him off with a blast of wind. Of course, she wasn't

45

anywhere close. She was back in her old home safe from the perils of misadventures.

Brownies like Madam Brown, small creatures who assume the role of caretakers for their chosen or contracted domains, had skills Olaf could use. If the river-troll could engage the services of a brownie, his whole realm would be a lot drier, less fishy smelling, and better managed. Most rule with tiny blue fists and a lot of sass. Thus, free from the day-to-day maintenance of his realm, Olaf could use his time to concentrate on goblins, or whatever came up next. He might even suggest it before leaving.

"Now be I showing you the real problem," said Olaf.

Christoffer jerked his thumb over his shoulder. "As opposed to the goblins back there? What's worse than having them at your doorstep?"

"We not yet be verifying to whom their allegiance belongs. They be pests, nothing more."

"Do you have a guess?" asked Christoffer, before warning, "Don't say dragon."

Olaf raised an eyebrow. "I not *not* be saying dragon, but it could be a hag, or banshees, or mares, or hulders, or mountain-trolls, or someone else I not be imagining."

"That doesn't really narrow it down."

"We be almost there. Hold your breath," said Olaf.

"You know, if this was going to be an all-day field trip, I should've called my mum first. She bugs out if I'm incommunicado. Not to mention my sisters are going to be disappointed." He pulled his cell phone from his bag, turned it on, and angled it toward the darkening sky. "Do you ever get service down here?"

Olaf rolled his eyes and walked across the room to the far side of the bubble. "This not be taking much longer. Olaf be taking you home after."

"Oh, okay then," Christoffer said, dropping his arm and tossing his phone back into the bag, hurrying to the troll's side.

At the bubble's barrier, the river-troll reached out with one long, slender finger and stroked the rippling wall with his nail. The air in the room evaporated like a vacuum, and the walls caved inward as the structure collapsed. Christoffer couldn't even yell in fright as all the air got sucked out. He clutched his aching throat.

And then it was over, and Christoffer gasped, inhaling great big gulps of air. "Warn a guy, would you? Jeez. That's some party trick."

The room where they now stood was cold, humid, frozen, and melting all at once. The water dripped in rivulets down the sides of a carved central island and stools. Olaf ran a hand along the surface, sluicing water over the edge. It landed with the sound of a loud slap.

"I don't get it," said Christoffer, rubbing his arms where gooseflesh rose up. He was definitely missing Madam Brown now, as he shook in his wet clothes.

"I be melting my domain," said Olaf. "All the places that be icy must thaw."

Christoffer blew on his hands to warm them. "Why?"

Olaf scrubbed his hand over his face tiredly. "My river be losing water."

"Your river's losing water? It didn't seem that way in Fredrikstad or even at the meeting of the Gjöll."

"I be melting my home to keep others from noticing the water level dropping. It be all I can do to hide it from Queen Helena. I tell her I be doing renovations, so she be not suspicious about being barred from these places in my home, but I be running out of time. If another river-troll be finding out, they could challenge me – say Olaf be unfit to guard – and I be losing my river. A troll who loses his river twice is no troll at all."

Christoffer kicked at the icy water under his feet, and guessed, "You're almost out of ice to melt."

"Yes," he said. "Soon human and mountain-troll cities be seeing what I be fighting for the last year. The Glomma be drying out and so be its lakes."

"If the humans notice, so, too, would other river-trolls. Why didn't you seek help?"

"I sought you," Olaf said.

Christoffer didn't know if he was touched or flummoxed. And if he was touched, was that weird? Olaf had kidnapped him once, after all. He wanted to know what kept Olaf from reaching out for aid sooner. Instead of asking, he focused on the more important topic. "You must have theories. What is causing this, and do you have a solution?"

"I not be finding the cause, and I be afraid of what that means."

"Not to mention the goblins on your doorstep," added Christoffer. He blew out a sigh and locked his gaze with the river-troll's. "So while you aren't saying dragon, you're thinking it, and you wanted to see if I drew the same conclusion before seeking Queen Helena's advice."

"Aye," said Olaf gruffly. "When I first be noticing it, I thought there might be a blockage somewhere, but no it not be that."

"Is it the result of a warmer winter than usual – less snow melt?"

"No, and it not be drought either."

Baffled, Christoffer ran a hand over his spiky hair. "Are humans diverting more of it for agriculture?"

"It be like some greedy giant be drinking it all," grumbled Olaf.

"I've seen it done before. It's possible," Christoffer ventured, remembering Pekka the Overwhelming's magic cups, which let the giant partake of beverages his size for the price of a human-size portion. "Especially if the giant had a malfunctioning item from the Hidden Gem. Nothing in Granny's comes with a warranty or satisfaction guarantee."

Olaf contemplated it, running his fingers through his wild fur-like hair. "It would be taking more than one thirsty giant to do this. A whole tribe perhaps," he said. "But they always be so careful to take only what the environment can sustain and nothing more."

"Do you think a tribe has gone rogue? Gotten greedy?"

A knock sounded, halting Olaf's response. His eyes widened, and he moaned in defeat. The knock came again, followed by a voice calling out, "Olaf, I know you're in there and that you have a guest. Let me in."

It was Queen Helena, and Olaf seemed to be perspiring under the pressure.

"You should not. It be very messy," the river-troll hedged.

"When have I cared?" Queen Helena asked. "If your friend can handle it, so can I."

"Contractor," whispered Christoffer. "Tell her I'm a contractor."

"I know it's you Christoffer," she said amused. "Let me in, or I will be forced to think you're hiding something from me."

Surrendering, Olaf made a circular motion with his finger, and Queen Helena's form materialized in the room with a short blast of warm air, causing Christoffer's ears to pop. To alleviate pressure, he yawned and wiggled a finger in his ear. Olaf might be able to move them between rooms in his house, but he couldn't do it as seamlessly or as subtly as when he moved by himself.

Queen Helena's appearance unnerved Christoffer. She lacked the vigor and force of presence he remembered. Her hair drooped, her clothes were disheveled, and her natural wheat and chestnut skin seemed almost sallow. Her erect figure wilted at the edges, and her purple eyes, which once burned with magic and power, glimmered like banked coals.

Is this how she looked *after* taking a break from dragons for over a year? It seemed impossible that the person he remembered at Aleks' coronation party could deteriorate like this. She had been so put together after going those ten rounds with Fritjof, that he'd assumed she'd recover the same way Zaria had after the chains sapping her power were removed. He now realized that for her daughter's and everyone's benefit, she must've used magic to hide the effects of the fight.

"How did you know it was me?" Christoffer asked, accepting a hug from the sorceress. "Also, how did you knock on a bubble?"

She pulled away to look at him. With a soft smile and a gentle touch under his chin to lift his face, she said, "There's only one you, and magic, of course."

"My voice gave me away didn't it," he grumped. "I'm the only one with this accent."

Her smile widened, as she turned away. Taking in Olaf and the rest of the room, her smile dropped. "I understand why you had this area blocked off. It's a wreck. Will you tell me what's going on, or will I have to pry it from you, my friend?"

"I be redecorating," Olaf insisted.

Queen Helena gave him an arched look. "You know I won't swallow that lie, Olaf. When have you ever redecorated?"

"That's why it needed to be done," said Christoffer, receiving a grateful glance from the river-troll.

She hummed noncommittedly. "Your new seating area was picked out by Queen Silje from a catalogue and delivered by a giant from Rubus the Golden's tribe. A special delivery made with the help of your cousin Bjarke and his dear *Ursula*. Want to try again? Maybe this time with the truth?"

Olaf grumbled under his breath, making Christoffer glad not to be in his shoes. As it was, there seemed to be a lot of people working together to help the river-troll – at least with redecorating – so he had to wonder why, when it came to the oddities and troubles he'd been experiencing, the troll didn't look for help sooner. Pride, perhaps? Or was he simply unused to having anyone he could count on?

Queen Helena sighed and touched the troll's knobby hands. "I was prepared to wait until you were ready to tell me, Olaf, but I think you shouldn't keep me waiting any longer."

The troll's hangdog expression drooped further. "I not be wanting to burden you. Already there be too much on your shoulders."

Queen Helena said kindly, "It's not a burden to listen to a friend."

Unable to stand the wait, Christoffer blurted, "It's the Glomma. There's something wrong."

Before she could ask for more details, Olaf launched into a description of his woes during the past year, and as he spoke, Queen Helena listened intently, interjecting once or twice to ask a question, but otherwise silent, absorbing all the facts. When he concluded, she continued to think in silence.

"I think I must return to the Under Realm," she said slowly, feeling out the words. "I believe something is afoot with the dragons that is affecting your river. There even may be signs of trouble in the Gjöll, which I should check."

"But the trees be good still," objected Olaf. "This be something different."

"You're not sure of that any more than I am," said Helena, bracing her hand against his shoulder. "I agree, this is a new tactic we haven't faced before, but if all options have been explored except this one, then it is obvious what I need to do."

"You look like a stiff breeze would knock you over," said Christoffer, not unkindly.

She laughed. "I have strength enough for this."

"You should be resting," Olaf said, taking her hand in his and looking earnestly into her eyes. "You still be recovering. Your magic —"

"Is fine, Olaf," she said gently, but firmly. "I appreciate your concern, but I think it's time we all head home. I will investigate, and you will help me warn the others that something new may be coming down the pike. Every preparation and precaution must be taken before it is too late."

"They not be listening to me," he said.

"They will if I give you this."

Queen Helena removed a ring from her finger and waved her hand to enlarge it, before carefully sliding it over Olaf's knuckle. The thick silver ring held an oval gem in a deep imperial purple shade entwined with stylized dragon heads. As Christoffer watched, the ring glinted like a star twinkling in the night sky, a clear sign of magic within the stone. Its presence on Olaf's finger would legitimize his words, and the trust inherent in the gift brought tears to the troll's eyes.

"Christoffer would you do me a favor?" she asked, giving an emotional Olaf a chance to recover himself.

"Anything," agreed Christoffer.

She pulled out a thick envelope and handed it to him. "Give this to Zaria. Tell her that I hope to see her soon, and that I love her."

"I will," he promised.

When she departed, Olaf gazed absently at the ring on his finger, rubbing it with the pad of his thumb. "This be... this be..."

"Unexpected?" offered Christoffer, hefting his envelope, resisting the urge to open it and look inside, for there was something in it that lent it weight. "We've got a lot of work to do."

Olaf snapped back to attention, dropping his hand. "I be needing to reach out to my cousin. You be needing to get home."

"Luckily, the two objectives coincide. How often does your cousin come to Fredrikstad?"

"Olaf not be knowing, but I be summoning him. Hold your breath," warned Olaf and Christoffer sucked in a large gulp of air just as the river-troll stroked the barrier, popping it, and the two dissolved into the sitting room.

"Thanks," Christoffer said, when he could breathe normally again. His eyes felt dry from the air evaporating and he rubbed them to bring back moisture.

When they arrived in the city later that day, Christoffer sprinted off with hardly a backward glance, leaving Olaf at the scrollwork bridge. The minute his mobile phone reconnected to the cellular network, it was ringing, and without looking at the caller identification he answered.

"Hey, mum," he panted.

"Christoffer Johansen, where are you?" his mother demanded. "Your sisters are about to go onstage."

"I'm almost there," he promised. "Homework. Distracted. Sorry."

There was silence, and when she spoke again, suspicion laced her words. "You were with Zaria?"

"No, Geirr," said Christoffer, with the inborn teenage intuition and subsequent self-preservation to offer up another name.

"Good," she said. "As Zaria and Henrik are here."

He let out a gusty sigh of relief for having guessed right. "Why do you always think I'm lying?" he complained.

"Aren't you?" she countered. "Look, as long as you're home on time, don't miss school, and aren't picked up by the police I can look the other way."

"I'm not lying," Christoffer insisted, cringing a little, as, even then, he lied.

"You're a good son," Emma said, making Christoffer feel worse. "And a good brother."

"The best," he agreed, sprinting around the block and dashing toward the small theater.

"They're flickering the lights," she warned. "Come inside and be quiet."

"Here," said Christoffer, banging open the lobby door and hanging up the phone.

Emma Johansen skewered him with her best withering military brass impression (giving Colonel Fierce a run for his money) and ushered him quickly through the interior doors to the auditorium and to their seats. He slid in beside his father and waved to Zaria and Henrik sitting on the other side.

She waved the program at him and Henrik inclined his head. Neither gave away by word or action that he'd been absent from school, but as the lights dimmed and the audience applauded the dance school owner to the stage, she mouthed, "Anything wrong?"

He shook his head and focused on the stage, clapping through the many acknowledgments and accolades. The theme for this performance was the northern lights, and the music and costumes were colorful and sharp like the edge of a winter wind. Several classes performed, and he dutifully clapped after each one; but, when his sisters' class shuffled on stage, he sat forward, drinking in their blue and green tutus and glittery headbands.

Several audience members cooed at the youngsters, who ranged in years from three to five. Their teacher lined up with them, and after one girl yanked out a wedgie, causing everyone to chuckle, the music began. His sisters, Ming Yue and Sying, also known as Moon and Star, started well, leading the group through curtseys and twirls before going off and doing their own thing.

Unsure if they'd forgotten the routine or were simply bored with it, Christoffer watched as Star flopped on her back and waved her feet in the air, admiring her ballet shoes, while Moon tried to stay with the group, but ended up doing all the moves in the opposite direction from everyone else. Their teacher helped Star to her feet and sweetly corrected Moon, so that she was back in alignment with the other girls.

Christoffer knew they were terrible, but they were so adorable that he felt they outshined the others, and their beaming smiles drew one from him. He glanced at his father and saw Zhuang watching with a soft pride. His mother gave his hand a firm squeeze before turning her gaze back to the stage, and he caught a shimmer of tears in her eyes.

"They were wonderful," said Zaria, grabbing refreshments in the lobby after the show.

Christoffer bought two roses and presented one to each of his sisters with a courtly flourish that they laughed at, but didn't really understand. They thought their brother was just being silly.

"Princess, you here," cried Moon, hugging Zaria about her knees.

She scooped the little girl up and rubbed noses with her. "I promised I would be, Moonbeam."

He'd told his sisters about his friend being a princess when she had come to visit one time and they'd been acting fussy. Their eyes had grown as big as saucers, and they'd peppered her with questions. Ever since, she'd been Princess, not Zaria, to them, and they treated her every word like it was gospel.

His father and Henrik were talking about what his friend's plans were for the future, and Christoffer was genuinely surprised to hear that Henrik was thinking of university. He thought the Stag Lord would want to be close to his people, but before he could dwell on that he remembered the envelope in his backpack and pulled it out, handing it to Zaria.

"What's this?" she asked, examining it curiously.

"It's from your mother," he said, taking Moon into his arms so she could open it.

"Why would mom give you this? I will see her when I get home."

"Not Merry," he whispered. "Queen Helena."

"When did you see her?"

"Today."

"Oh," she said in surprise. Prying the seal apart, she pulled out the sheet of paper and unfolded it. At its heart, was a thin, sharp, shard of metal. Zaria picked it up, catching his eye. She frowned at it and then him, hurt and suspicion in her voice. "Why did you see her?"

He shook his head and shrugged. "Olaf waylaid me this morning. It's a long story. What does she say?"

Zaria returned her attention to the letter and began reading. She gasped, dropping the paper and shard of metal, and covering her mouth. Christoffer set his sister down and bent over to pick up both items. Flipping the letter over, he read the short missive.

*Dearest Zaria,*

*I found this while putting to rights the Under Realm.*

*I know what happened to the sword. Common knowledge of this could be disastrous. <u>Nobody</u> is to know its fate.*

*You must replace it, daughter. It's imperative. Do it quickly and quietly.*

*Be careful. I love you.*

*Your mother,*

*Helena*

"It seems we got ourselves a Queen's quest," he mused, handing both letter and sword shard back to her. "You should put that away before anyone sees."

She hurried to do so, folding up the note and stuffing it in her pocket, before she slipped the metal shard into her purse and snapped it shut. It took her a moment more to school her features back into a pleasant mien in order to say goodnight to his parents and kiss his sisters goodbye. She gathered Henrik and shuffled him through the crowd, with a pointed, anxious look back at Christoffer.

While it was clear she was uneasy about the directive from her mother, Christoffer could hardly wait to gather up the team and venture forth. The perks of being a sidekick meant one never really had to worry about the difficult stuff, and the journey held all the fun. He waved goodnight, knowing tomorrow the hero's quest would begin.

# Chapter Three: The Party Underworlds

Filip and Aleks showed up at his door the next day. His mum answered, keeping Star from rushing outside, while Moon clung to her leg. "Boys, what are you doing here so early?" she asked, alarm – and suspicion – in her voice.

Christoffer appeared behind his mum with Defender at his heels. He dragged his friends past the threshold into the house. "They're here to discuss a school project that's due this morning."

"Why didn't you work on it yesterday after the recital?" she asked, sending them a skeptical look.

"We have an hour before school," explained Aleks, careful to keep his fangs hidden. "We just need to check some references."

"Fine. Don't be late." She reached for his bright coppery hair. Aleks swerved the touch, anxiously patting down his hair to cover his pointy fey ears. "Young man, you need a haircut. I'm sure this mop is giving your mother fits."

He countered with a sheepish, "My girlfriend likes it."

"That explains it," she said with amusement. "Tell me more about her."

Sniffing the air, Filip interrupted, "Are those bao buns, Mrs. Johansen?"

Christoffer grinned and guided his friends into the steamy kitchen. "Take your pick, there's plenty."

"Which ones are which?" asked Aleks, peering under the lids of the different bamboo steamers.

Pointing as he spoke, Christoffer highlighted, "These are bacon and egg, those are spinach and salmon, and these here are sausage and cheese."

"These are delicious, Mrs. Johansen," Filip moaned, chowing down. "You make the best food. Adopt me."

"I made them with some help," she said, settling the twins down at the table to eat rice porridge.

"Mum's teaching me to cook, so I don't starve at university," Christoffer explained, grabbing a full steamer and a handful of buns from the other baskets, carrying them to his room. Defender followed him loyally every step, hopeful for a handout or a dropped treat.

"In that case, mate, I'm officially claiming you as my roommate," Filip told him, snatching at another steamed bun.

"No way, not with how you snore," Christoffer joked, waiting for Defender to leap up onto the bed.

"What? Not going to ask Zaria to move into an apartment with you?" teased Aleks.

Filip's ears went bright red as he blushed. "I can't ask her to do that. Her dad would murder me and bury the body. He doesn't know about dragons, but he'd somehow make you think they did it."

Aleks grinned conspiratorially. "Ah, the joys of military father-in-laws. I know them well."

"I – I – I," spluttered Filip.

The fairy king nudged him. "Fox got your tongue?"

"We're not engaged like you and Saskia," Filip managed to choke out, red in the face.

"We're not engaged," reminded Aleks.

"*Yet*," added Christoffer laughingly, while dropping the buns on his desk. "Just give it a little time, and you will be. You're basically engaged to be engaged."

Throwing himself onto his bed, he hooked Defender with one arm around the neck and wrestled with him. The border collie woofed happily, and after a quick scratch behind the ears and a stern command to wait, Christoffer proffered the expected treat – half a bun with bacon and egg.

Filip sat at the veneer-worn desk chair, and Aleks leaned against the windowsill, crowding the small room. Aleks picked apart one of the buns, blowing on his fingers as he juggled it. Fussing with food, they waited until his mother's footsteps faded back toward the kitchen.

Kicking the bag by his feet, Christoffer spoke first. "I'm all packed. When do we plan to leave?"

Filip glanced at the open door. "Sh... your mom might hear."

He waved away his friend's concern. "Star and Moon are claiming her attention. They're cute, but little she-devils to get ready in the morning. Mum gets one ready only to have the other undo everything and run around screaming. She'll be taking them off to daycare shortly and won't have time to eavesdrop."

Filip eyed the doorway, doubt etched across his features. "You've only just been cleared for no curfew and checking in once every four hours."

"If only you were kidding," Christoffer said, grinning unconcernedly. "Luckily, I persuaded them to let me date. That there is the bigger accomplishment."

"As long as your grades don't slip," reminded Aleks.

"And have they?" admonished Christoffer. "No, they haven't. Besides, my relatively new freedom is not what you're here to discuss. Did Zaria tell you what Helena wrote?"

Filip offered Aleks the steam basket, before setting it down and closing the lid. He nodded carefully. "What I don't get, though, is why give an order but not any instruction. How do we fix *it*? It's not like superglue is going to work."

The "it" he stressed being the Drakeland Sword.

"I think we're going to have to reach out to allies," said Aleks thoughtfully.

"We're not supposed to tell anyone," Filip reminded, giving him a firm look. "We shouldn't get Zaria into more trouble."

His changeling friend rolled his eyes. For being king over all of Niffleheim he could still behave in a juvenile manner. Christoffer was glad his friend's elevated status hadn't turned him into someone he wasn't. The eye roll was proof that his friend hadn't outgrown them and that meant more than words could express. Christoffer had no intention of being left behind.

"Of course we don't tell them," Aleks retorted. "We need to learn more about how it was fashioned in the first place. Someone created it."

Christoffer perked up. "Dwarves, right? I mean, it makes sense because of the special ore."

Filip rubbed his belly and stretched. "I think that's right. King Flein mentioned something back when we first got the sw – it."

"I really don't want to deal with dwarves," grumped Aleks. "It's been a pain sorting everything out since killing Fritjof. King Flein is anxious to find a way to heal the rift and clear his debt. He's constantly sending envoys. I even got an invite to Prince Floki's trial, which I'm sending Sivert to oversee."

"Delegating is tough," said Christoffer wisely, a twinkle in his eye.

"You jest, because you don't realize all the demands on my attention. If it wasn't for Nori, Saskia, and Sivert I'd never be able to leave Niffleheim. Thank God they're on my side, or I'd be a basket case."

"So, you're dwarved-out?" asked Christoffer, accepting Aleks' nod.

"You might not have a choice, mate," said Filip. "It sounds like our only lead."

"We'll be glad you have that debt then," said Christoffer, clapping his wary friend on the back.

"Christoffer, boys, you need to get going or you'll be late," warned Emma, poking her head in the room. "Don't forget your father wants you home right after school today to help him paint the living room."

"It's Wednesday mum, that's not even logical. Why not wait 'til the weekend?"

She glanced at his friends. "Don't you have a dance? Sounds like you're trying to get out of helping your father. You know the rules."

"Fine, fine. I'll be there," Christoffer relented, grievance clear in his voice. He shooed her out of his room, and as soon as the door shut, he muttered to Aleks, "Please tell me you're activating the stargazer today before school or after, honestly I don't care when."

"You really do want to get out of chores," Filip said knowingly.

"Oh poo, it's not like you haven't skipped out on family duties before."

"Poo?" asked Aleks, smirking.

Christoffer rolled his eyes. "Poo. My sisters repeat everything these days. If I say anything stronger, my mother will blister my ears."

"Doesn't that defeat the purpose?" asked Filip.

He shrugged. "You know what I mean. I remember your mum chasing after you once. A regular old banshee she was."

Filip held up his hands in surrender. "Fair enough, mate. Let's grab our stuff and go."

"We're meeting everybody at the bridge," said Aleks. "Zaria spoke to Olaf, and he's prepared to help us get where we need to go, so long as it doesn't keep him from his new duties."

"I guess we're going where he's going then," said Christoffer, slinging his backpack over his shoulder. He eyed Filip's single bag. "Traveling light this time?"

He nodded. "Having two packs didn't help me at all before, and I still had to replace stuff. Mum wasn't happy about that one bit."

On the way out, Christoffer hugged his mum with one arm and ruffled his sisters' hair affectionately. "Bye-bye jellybeans," he told them. "See you later, Mum," he added.

"Have a good day at school. I'll be leaving with the girls soon," she said. "Tell your brother you love him."

"I lub you!" they chorused.

"I love you, too," he said to all three. "Stay, be a good boy," he told Defender, whose tail had stopped wagging.

Refusing to capitulate to those sad canine eyes, he waved goodbye, and closed the front door. His step light, he followed his friends to the infamous bridge and its water-dwelling inhabitant. If it wasn't for the river-troll, none of them would have ventured out into the wonders of magical Norway all those years ago, as Aleks had been quite content to live his days out as a human, and Zaria had no idea she was a sorceress with magical powers. Who knew that someday the sinister pirate-talking villain would be an ally and not an enemy? Funny how things changed.

His mobile phone began buzzing, and he fished it out of his pocket. The face on the screen was his mother. "Mum? Is everything all right? Did I forget something?"

Aleks and Filip stopped walking, looking back at him. He held up a finger.

"Christoffer, your dog got loose," she announced, panic stricken. "I was getting the girls out to the car and he snuck around me."

"Is he nearby? I'll come get him," he said, waving his friends ahead and turning back.

"He ran off," Emma said, her voice tight with emotion. "I tried calling him, but he doesn't listen to me. I can't leave your sisters."

Christoffer broke into a loping run. "I'll find him, mum, you take the girls and go. If you see him while driving, call me."

"Are you sure?" she asked. "I feel like I should be looking."

"I've got to go, mum, and so do you. I'll call you when I find him," he said between controlled breaths as he turned the corner. Spying a familiar shaggy coat and lopsided toothy grin, he slowed. "Actually, mum, Defender found me."

"You see him?" Emma said, relief flooding her voice. "He's a bad boy, you need to lock him up. That little escape artist nearly gave me a –"

Christoffer knelt down and scratched behind Defender's ears, cooing, "Who's my little escape artist? Huh? Is that you? Are you my good boy?"

"Make sure you take him home before going to school," his mother said with an affectionate sigh. "You spoil him."

"Okay, mum, bye," he said, hanging up. He went back to scratching and giving belly rubs as Defender hammed it up, tongue lolling sideways. "You're pleased with yourself, aren't you?" He got a woof in response and a big kiss. He laughed, shoving the dog away and stood. "Defender, heel."

He did, immediately falling into line, but instead of going home, Christoffer turned and trekked back toward his waiting friends. Sensing the adventure, Defender woofed happily and gazed slavishly up at him. "You just wanted to go on the adventure, didn't you? You didn't want to be left behind, not this time. No sir, not you, you're the wandering kind."

"You're not bringing him with us, are you?" asked Aleks, when the two stopped beside them.

Christoffer looked down at his grinning dog and shrugged. "Why not?"

"He could get hurt," Aleks said.

"You got Airi; besides, Defender can hold his own."

"Airi is a white raven; she's smart, and she can fly."

Filip leaned over and petted the dog. "You're smart, ol' boy, aren't you?"

"The smartest," Christoffer agreed. "Look how he tracked me down just now."

"If you're cool with it, I'm cool with it," Filip said to them both.

Aleks pursed his lips a moue of disapproval, but nodded his consent. "Fine, let's catch up to the others. They're probably wondering where we're at."

"Nah," said Christoffer. "They probably think my mum is tying me down to a chair so she knows where I am at all times."

"Your mom really isn't that bad anymore," Filip said. "She's actually pretty cool."

"You're just in love with her bao buns," quipped Christoffer.

When they reached the scrollwork bridge, the rest of the motley group was there waiting with their scaly friend. Olaf and Henrik stood side by side nearly at the same height. He could see that Henrik was a hair taller, even without his cloak, which sat wrapped in a bundle by his feet. The ellefolken prince had grown visibly after working another summer for the witch of the woods. Two more summers would fulfill his father's bargain with her. Christoffer wondered what would happen then for the Stag Lord.

Off to the side, leaning against the metal railing, Zaria and Geirr were swapping an oversized hot bun between them, taking generous bites and licking icing off their fingers. The sight and smell didn't appeal at the moment. He'd already eaten enough for a small army.

Even still, that didn't prevent him from asking, "Did you save any for me?"

"You want some?" Zaria offered, waving the bun by its crinkle paper. Her heavy chocolate-brown hair was styled in a way that would make Rapunzel envious, and he should know, because his sisters watched the movie on repeat.

"Not even a little, but Defender might," he teased, as his dog left him and raced over to her.

He sat, giving her food the most glistening soft doggie eyes. Zaria's gaze met his above the woeful, furry face, and she shook her head. "He's too cute for his own good. Geirr you take the bun before I give in and give the beggar what he wants."

Geirr laughed and accepted the bun, eating the rest of it quickly. His friend had relaxed his wardrobe over the years, swapping his customary buttoned-down, hemmed, and collared wear for new indigo jeans, sans belt, with a logo- and wrinkle-free T-shirt in a vibrant pink, which suited his rich, mocha-like complexion well and stretched across newly gained muscles from the gym.

"Did you contact your cousin?" asked Christoffer, turning to Olaf.

The river-troll nodded. "He be meeting me where be his territory and mine join in two days. With his help I be getting to the High Court of Jötunheim to gain an audience with Oskar the Elevated."

The sound of Olaf's voice drew Defender's attention, and the border collie immediately stilled, his head cocked and ears pricked to attention. He wolfed, barking loudly, his tail cautiously wagging side to side. Olaf reached into his pants' pocket and pulled out a small meaty treat. Defender's tail wagged furiously. He looked up at Christoffer, whining.

"All right, traitor. Go," he said affectionately. Defender bounded over and gobbled the treat, before sniffing all around Olaf curiously.

"Are we here for another boat?" asked Filip, wrapping an arm around Zaria's shoulders and giving her a brief hug hello.

"What we need is a bubble," said Christoffer. "Olaf and I reached the edge of Gloomwood Forest in a matter of hours. Those things move fast."

"Only when I be in them, too," cautioned Olaf, nudging a persistent, wet, black nose out of his crotch area. "Without my magic pushing the bubble along, you be subject to the whims of the river. Moving one from a distance be more draining to me and me powers than be wise at the moment."

"My mother's task is very urgent, but I don't know where to start with it," Zaria said, leaning against Filip and training her gaze on the troll. "Did she mention it to you?"

Olaf shook his head. "Queen Helena not be telling me what she be needing of you. Instead, I be fulfilling another task for her."

"He's to warn all the kingdoms that there may be a new dragon on the prowl," explained Christoffer, gesturing to the river-troll's webbed fingers. "She gave him a ring to prove his words."

"What task be she giving the little princess?" asked Olaf. "I be helping how I can."

"She specifically told me not to tell anyone," Zaria said with regret.

Olaf flinched, but nodded, rubbing the ring to sooth the sting of her words. Christoffer frowned at his feet. If Helena trusted the river-troll enough to impart the news of a new dragon threat to the kingdoms, why hadn't she trusted him with the knowledge of the sword? Was Zaria right to keep it from Olaf or had Helena expected her daughter to lean on the river-troll? He didn't know, but perhaps old scars were still healing beneath the placid surface of forgiveness.

"Some things one best be doing in secret," Olaf said, looking away and dropping his hand. "Olaf be willing to take everyone by bubble. There be enough time to get there and back before meeting Bjarke, but Princess need be telling me where to go."

Zaria glanced at Henrik and Aleks. "Do you have any idea where to start?"

Aleks frowned. "Who might know something that we can trust?"

"Trust," murmured Geirr. "That is the crux of it. Who can we trust?"

"The witch of the woods might know something," Henrik said, thinking it through. "She may have seen something or heard something of import."

Aleks nodded sagely, keen to the idea. "We wouldn't have to tell her much of anything in return."

"Do we have anything to offer as bargain or barter?" asked Geirr.

Zaria gripped the edge of her rucksack. "What about a future boon? Didn't Hector do that?"

Henrik leaned over and grabbed his cloak, unraveling the ropes around it. "My father made many bargains including ones like you say. If what we have on hand isn't to her liking, we can find something else."

"To the witch then?" asked Christoffer, excitement growing in him.

"The witch be always a good beginning place," said Olaf. "It be good to bring the hound."

"Defender? How come?" asked Filip.

"There be goblins," he said. "They be all over the forest. You not be walking anywhere without encountering a few." He waved a hand over the water and beckoned them closer. "Be you ready to travel to Gloomwood?"

Christoffer spied the whirlpool over the side of the bridge. His friends' disconcerted expressions tickled his funny bone. With a laugh he clambered up onto the railing beside Olaf. When Henrik grimaced, extremely uncomfortable with the upcoming jump, and twisting his cloak in his hands, Christoffer canted his head searchingly.

"What's the matter?" he asked.

Henrik crossed his arms, and shook his head. "It's nothing."

Christoffer knew it wasn't nothing. Unlike the others, he knew all too well what sort of memories might haunt the Stag Lord. He also knew that his friend wouldn't want Zaria feeling guilty about a long ago mistake. He stretched out his hand, and said, "It'll be different down there this time. Trust me."

Hesitantly, Henrik grabbed his hand and even accepted Olaf's assistance. Up on the rail he hunched forward, staring into the whirling abyss. His brilliant blue eyes darted once behind him to gaze at Zaria.

"Come on in, the water's fine," chirped Christoffer, and stepped off over the ledge.

In the water, he felt, rather than saw, Henrik follow. The rush of bubbles and fleeting water disturbance repeated several more times, as his friends rushed to join. The whirlpool deposited them with a splash into the middle of Olaf's living room and Christoffer grinned at their gasps of shock and awe, for once being the guide instead of the guided.

"You know, you could have taken this guy with you, instead of leaving him for us," Aleks said drily, appearing last and clutching a wriggling and bucking Defender. He let the dog go as gently as possible. Using Aleks' arms for a launchpad, the dog jumped away, leaving raw angry lines from his hind paws.

"Oops," said Christoffer. Then, stridently, "Defender, no!"

But it was too late; he was out of reach. Christoffer cringed under Zaria's glare as his dog did an all over body shake, spraying her with more water. He grabbed Defender and pulled him away, as she accepted a towel from Henrik and began drying her arms, neck, and face. She said nothing, but her eyes sparkled with dangerous intent.

Christoffer cast a pleading look toward Olaf. "Tell me, are we there yet?"

"That was rhetorical," said Geirr, when Olaf opened his mouth to respond.

Using the distraction to her advantage, Zaria attacked, tickling Christoffer into submission. Laughing, he wasn't surprised when his pleas for aid were unmet. Even Defender seemed to have turned against him, excited by the game and Zaria's obvious triumph.

"No fair," he wheezed, rolling away.

"Fair," cried the others, laughing.

"Okay, okay," Christoffer said, breaking free of Zaria's clutches. "Let's turn on the stargazer. I'd really rather my mother didn't find out we're not in school today. Getting caught playing hooky twice would be my undoing."

# Chapter Four: Of Scavengers and Ghouls

Olaf dumped them out as close to Gloomwood Forest as he could take them through his territory. The Gjǫll and Glomma rivers sparkled under the early evening light of stars. His royal friends bid the river-troll *adieu* and thanked him again for his troubles.

Happy for new scents, Defender raced off to mark his territory on the surrounding trees. Olaf sneered, disgusted. "Be it any wonder your hound still be able to urinate."

Christoffer shrugged, tucking his hands into his pockets. "What can I say? He's a dog – a male dog at that. They pee on everything."

"Never again," muttered Olaf, spitting on the ground. "That beast of yours is a menace."

Defender had loved Olaf's underwater realm and had gone around marking everything he could find, for their fishy, outdoor smells called to him like nothing else. Christoffer and the others had tried to stop him from doing it, but after ten minutes chasing him around, which essentially made a game of it for him, they had resigned themselves. He had peed on everything from a patch of sand that beckoned his attention to the furniture itself.

At first, Christoffer was horrified, but Defender soon began to mark on empty, squeezing out droplets, and the humor of the situation got to him. He couldn't help but feel that his revenge for being kidnapped had been completed by his canine companion. Judging by the quietly amused gaze of Henrik, he thought the Stag Lord must have felt so, too.

"This be where Olaf say goodbye, Princess," said the troll, shaking out his long hair and walking back toward the water's edge.

"Good luck with your ambassador duties," Zaria said, waving goodbye, as Filip came over and shouldered her bag. She smiled happily at him.

"Aye, and luck be to you Princess for your own task."

They stood together on the shoreline watching as Olaf slipped back into the Glomma until only his long nose and yellow eyes glowed above the waterline. Clouds scuttled overhead, darkening the night sky, and when they drifted away, he was gone, and the waters lapped over the spot where he'd been.

"Water we waiting for? Let's go," Christoffer spouted, cracking a grin. As his friends collected their gear and fished out lanterns, his face fell. "Nothing, guys? Really?"

Geirr looked up and smirked. "Your puns are as lame as your face."

"I could give you a pity laugh," offered Filip, snickering as Aleks nodded with him.

Christoffer pouted. "I hate you all so much."

"It was very clever," Zaria offered.

He groaned. "Oh, that's so much worse. Stop, okay, stop. You don't deserve my witticisms anyway."

"If you call that wit, I truly wonder about you," said Henrik, cottoning on to the mood of the others.

With feigned irritation, Christoffer huffed, "See if I provide comic relief to you drudges in the future."

"Is he offering to be silent?" Aleks asked, delighted.

"Will wonders never cease?" joked Geirr.

Filip grinned and nudged Henrik, waggling his eyebrows. "Our ears are saved!"

"None of you are friends," Christoffer grumbled, stomping after his dog. "At least my dog loves me."

Zaria glared at everyone, but only Henrik and Filip appeared to be cowed. She turned and ran after him until he slowed down. "Of course we love you, Christoffer. They're just ribbing you. Forget them."

Henrik sighed and shook out his damp cloak. He slung it across his shoulders and stood the hood up. "We've got a long night ahead of us, if we plan to see the witch before the world ends."

"Don't be so cheery. We can't take any more comedy tonight," Geirr said drolly.

"What's funny about the world ending?" Henrik asked, furrowing his brow.

Geirr sighed. "Christoffer would've gotten that one."

Hearing his name, Christoffer glanced up from loving on Defender and gave Geirr a thumbs up. The two boys grinned conspiratorially, and all was well. Zaria looked on them with fond exasperation, as Christoffer looped an arm around her shoulders and steered her back to the others, his dog faithfully on their heels.

The long hike through the night was broken when a soft rolling fog drifted across the ground. Expecting winter-wyverns, Christoffer looked up and spied instead the dark shape of the Gjallarbrú – a covered bridge into the Under Realm – appearing out of the mist. Its golden roof glinted occasionally, as starlight penetrated the rising fog.

"We can take a rest here," Zaria said, her step quickening in anticipation. "I can conjure us some food. What does everyone want to eat?"

"That sounds amazing, Zar-Zar. I'm famished," Filip said, pressing a kiss to her temple and squeezing her hand before slinging their bags off his shoulder.

As they approached the bridge, Henrik tensed, stopping them from getting any closer. "Something's wrong," he murmured. "There should be guards here. Where are the elves?"

"Maybe they're on an extended bathroom break?" Christoffer suggested.

"I hope that's all it is," muttered Aleks, gazing about warily, his hand inching toward his bow.

"Do you hear that?" Filip asked, pitching his voice above the river's babble.

Christoffer and the others listened intently. Something scraped in the night. It was almost rhythmic – *scritch, scritch,* pause, *scritch, scritch, scritch,* pause, *scritch, scritch.* On it went, jarring everyone's nerves. Geirr aimed his flashlight toward the trees, searching for the source. Henrik cast his beam along the shoreline.

Purple sparks of magic gathered at Zaria's fingertips, brightening the scene. Voice strangled, she whispered, "I don't think the guards are on a bathroom break."

In the shadows of the bridge's pilings a hunched silhouette moved restlessly and unnaturally. As Zaria's magic pulsed, the shape broke apart revealing a quintet of goblins. It took a moment for Christoffer to understand what he was seeing under the purple haze of her magic.

"Is that – is that – is…" Geirr stammered, unable to finish his sentence.

The goblins' meal lay torn in pieces between them. The bloody meat slowly took shape and Christoffer realized with horror that it was the remnants of someone's face and limbs. Bile rose hard and fast and he turned aside to cast up his accounts.

"Get back!" shouted Henrik, causing Defender to bark excitedly. He unsheathed his sword and shifted into a fighting stance.

Zaria threw a fireball, and the goblins scattered, but some were not fast enough. Two caught on fire, and began screaming hideous unearthly sounds, making banshees far and wide proud. They beat themselves and threw themselves at the ground, but neither tried to get in the water, the most obvious source of relief.

The Gjöll once belonged to Olaf before he'd given it back to itself to protect the Under Realm. Being a wild river once more, it was protected by wild magic. Any creature with magic in its veins who dared to cross it would die, as its magic was bled out to feed the river. It was the fate that nearly destroyed Aleks when facing down Fritjof. He survived due to his clever white raven's quick thinking and a bond to a larger source of magic than even the river could drain.

"Fire!" one of the goblins hissed, rearing back from his fellow creature.

"Dog! Dog! Dog!" cried the one beside it frantically.

Christoffer held onto Defender's growling form, keeping him back from the fight. The dog was going berserk, lunging forward and snapping its jaws. He frothed in his struggle to reach them, desperate to protect his master and those he considered pack members.

"Don't, Defender," he commanded. "Quiet."

His words were ignored.

Henrik, Filip, and Geirr raced into the fold, wielding swords. Aleks and Zaria provided range support on the sides. Christoffer gripped the hilt of a dagger and hugged Defender close, wishing to be in the heat of battle, but staying out of it for practicality's sake.

Weapons flashed in the night – a ballet of metal, wood, and fire. The two goblins on fire died gasping in pain, their acrid burning flesh singeing the hairs of Christoffer's nostrils. The other three vanished into the forest, their meal forgotten in their desire to escape into the murky gloom.

In the quiet aftermath, his friends' panting breaths added to the fog of the night. Blood dripped from a cut on Filip's elbow. More dripped from his blade, but instead of red it shone in the night like an oil slick. Through it all, Defender barked, ears and nose pricked for danger, his sights set on where the goblins had escaped.

Zaria sank next to one of the bodies, her hand covering her mouth. She whispered, reaching out with a trembling hand, "These poor elves."

Henrik stood beside her, his face a mask, completely devoid of expression. "I don't recognize them," he said.

"How could anyone?" asked Christoffer weakly, finally letting Defender go when the border collie stopped barking.

He loped over to the bodies, sniffing. Zaria pushed his muzzle away. "No," she said firmly and Defender sat on his heels.

"We need to report this to Queen Silje," Aleks said, reaching for his belt.

Henrik did the same and both pulled out a gjallarhorn. To Christoffer they looked identical at first glance, but the designs on their bands and mouth pieces were different. Henrik's held a pattern of abstract curlicues, while Aleks' looked more like stylized feathers. He was really putting the raven imagery everywhere, it seemed.

Aleks gestured with his horn. "You go ahead. I've not gotten the knack of this thing yet. My gjallarhorn sounds like a wounded animal. I can never seem to call up the right person."

"If you have one of those, why do you need Airi?" asked Filip curiously.

"The gjallarhorn is less secure," Aleks said, stuffing his back into its sheath on his belt. "You never know who is listening or interfering. Remember how Fritjof caused it to go haywire?"

Filip said, "I guess what it lacks in security, it makes up for in speed."

"I cannot confirm your statement, or Airi will scratch my eyes out," Aleks joked. "She's the superior messenger and must always hold said title."

Henrik cleared his throat and they fell silent as he brought the horn to his lips and blew into it. A short series of trilling notes glistened in the air like dew. When their echoes faded, Queen Silje's holographic form appeared. It looked like she was in bed and hardly awake. Her platinum hair gleamed, even tied in knots and covered by a kerchief.

"Who dares to disturb me while I rest? Do you know what time it is?" she demanded, prying her eyes open and blinking owlishly at them.

"My apologies, your highness," Henrik said, bowing. "I understand the lateness of the hour, but the matter is most urgent."

"Stag Lord?" she asked, scrubbing her eyes.

"It is I," he confirmed.

"Is that Princess Zaria and King Aleks beside you?"

"Yes, now to the difficult news —"

"And beyond them, their human friends, yes? Is that Geirr who cleverly defeated Olaf on the Gjallarbrú three years ago?"

"Good evening, Queen Silje," Geirr called out, slightly bashful and full of pride.

Christoffer envied his friend the recognition he'd won. To have a queen from the magical realms remember your name and the deeds you'd done was true fame. There was Queen Helena of course, who had remembered him. He decided that didn't count for she was related to one of his friends. That connection made her a more invested party.

"Queen Silje, the matter at hand is most terrible and infinitely sorrowful."

Her gaze snapped back to Henrik's. Her lilting soprano voice took on a new authoritative edge. "I am listening. Proceed."

"It is with deepest condolences that I must inform you that your guards at the Gjallarbrú are dead."

"Dead? Impossible."

"I'm afraid it is true," Zaria said, coming to stand beside Henrik. The edges of his white cloak seemed to curl around her, seeking comfort.

"Explain," she commanded.

Zaria looked helplessly at Henrik, but he was swallowing thickly and unable to speak. Aleks stepped up and gestured at the river's bank. "We found a group of goblins feasting on their remains."

"But goblins are scavengers, not predators," Silje protested. "Are you saying they killed my guards?"

"They were abnormally aggressive," Henrik managed.

"However," Zaria interrupted. "We can't confirm whether or not they killed your elves, or if they found them that way."

Thoughts ticked behind Queen Silje's eyes as she pondered what they said. She began removing the ties from her hair, letting the curling strands fall. She swung her legs over the side of her bed and stood and the holographic form of her bed winked out.

"I will send reinforcements immediately, and an investigation team. Has your mother been informed, Princess Zaria?"

"We reached out to you first," Filip said.

"Good. I will inform Queen Helena, just as soon as I can deliver to her a more thorough report. Where are the goblins now?"

Christoffer looked down at the burnt remains of the bodies. He said, "We killed two, and three more ran off into the woods."

"Leave the bodies," Silje instructed.

"But your highness, that's not a good idea," interjected Henrik, startled. "You know what can happen if the goblins return."

"I'm willing to find out how desperate they are," she said, venom in her words.

"What can happen?" asked Aleks. "What do you mean? Should we stay until your elves arrive?"

"No need, they will be there within a few hours. Good-bye, children, I must let you go and take care of things from my side."

The connection ended, and she disappeared. Henrik jerked on the hood of his antlered cloak and kicked at the ground. "We should set the bodies alight and ensure they're nothing but ashes. She's foolish to risk their compatriots returning."

"Anyone else hate that we keep getting called children by the adults?" Geirr grumbled.

Christoffer crossed his arms. "It's not the adults taking care of dragons."

Zaria laid a gentle hand on his forearm. "Silje and the others, they're doing what they can – protecting as they know best. Isn't it nice that they see us as children? They don't expect us to confront dragons."

Geirr said darkly, "It's still us that meets them."

"Not the issue right now," Aleks said, twisting his raven cuff absently around and around on his wrist.

"No," agreed Filip. "Henrik is about to explain why leaving goblin bodies exposed to the elements is a stupid idea."

"Ghouls," he bit out, kicking the dirt again.

Christoffer's eyes widened and Defender whined in the night, unhappy with all the tension. He said, "Ghouls, what do they have to do with the price of dragon scales in Malmdor?"

Henrik dropped to his haunches next to his bag and began rifling through it. "When goblins eat the flesh of their own kind they become cursed... diseased. Their green skin bleaches of color, graying like ashes in a fire. They go from being part of a pack to being loners, from scavengers to monsters, from eating meat to eating rotting corpses, from paralyzing bites to killing ones."

"They haunt graveyards," Filip guessed, rubbing his forearms. Henrik inclined his head.

"It's bad then, isn't it, that I think they smell like roast chicken," Christoffer said, wrinkling his nose in distaste even as his stomach growled.

Geirr groaned, covering his face. "I did not need that imagery."

"Oh, come on, man," Christoffer defended. "You've got to be thinking it, too. They smell like barbeque."

"Do goblins normally eat their own kind?" Zaria murmured, training her gaze on the shadowy trees.

Henrik shook his head, straightening up, his bag in one hand and a lighter in the other. "No, they don't."

"Only ones desperate enough to do so," Aleks mused. "Which is why Queen Silje wants their remains exposed. She's searching for clues."

Filip poked one gingerly with his foot. "Do we leave them, then, like she asked?"

Henrik stared at Zaria. "I leave that up to you, Princess."

"Just to be clear, the dead goblins don't rise up as ghouls, correct?" Christoffer felt inclined to ask.

Henrik leaned away horrified. "Heaven forbid, no."

"Okay then," he said, looking to the others. "I say we leave them, just as the elf queen asked. It's not like we're risking a zombie apocalypse."

Aleks arched an eyebrow. "I'm glad we're not a superstitious lot, or that would be some heavy foreshadowing, right there."

Christoffer grinned and threw Zaria a wink. "And imagine that's *only* the worst thing that can happen."

Zaria shook her head fondly at him and hiked up her bag on her shoulder. "I agree with Christoffer, but if it's all the same to you guys, I would like to get out of here. We can eat on the trail."

Incredulous, Aleks blurted out, "You can eat?"

She swallowed thickly. "Not right now, with the sight and the smell, but we will need to eat something to keep our energies up."

"I still say it smells like chicken," said Christoffer, rubbing the bridge of his nose.

Grimacing, Geirr said, "I think we should listen to Henrik. Goblins are bad enough; we don't need to be running across ghouls, too. We should stay, and eat after taking care of things here."

"I don't care either way," said Aleks. "I wouldn't mind the rest. What do you think Filip?"

The blond teen shrugged. "Whatever Zaria wants to do is fine with me, just so long as I get a hot fudge ice cream cone for dessert. I need something sweet to remind me it's not all blood and gore."

"With extra hot fudge?" she asked, looking a tad wan.

Geirr and Aleks groaned in unison as that essentially sealed the deal, shouldered their bags, and started trudging along the Gjöll.

"At least I'm not the only one left with an appetite," said Christoffer. "That's a small comfort."

Henrik flicked the lighter thrice, letting it catch. Christoffer watched as he stared at the bodies. Their gazes met and the ellefolken prince snapped the lighter shut, stuffing it into his jeans pocket. Unhappy with the group's decision, he brooded in the background.

Taking one last look at the pointed roof of the Gjallarbrú behind him, Christoffer hummed to himself a soft, misshapen rhyme. For a time, he knew not what it reminded him of and kept repeating it under his breath; but the tune became more and more familiar, bringing with it the words. To please himself, he changed them and softly sung.

*"The time has come," the Stag Lord said,*

*"To talk of many rules:*

*Of elves — and guards — and crimson fire —*

*Of scavengers — and ghouls —*

*And why the dark begins to creep —*

*And whether queens are fools."'*

It was a good thing Aleks hadn't heard him, or for that matter any of the others. The only one to have heard didn't understand a word. Defender muttered a tired woof, and pressed against his legs. Christoffer scratched his head in commiseration and the two continued on through the long night with nary another ghoul, brownie, banshee, or goblin in sight.

# Chapter Five: The Witch's Checkpoint

To Christoffer the lichen-covered archway brought instant relief and a rush of energy. The anticipation of sitting down and freeing his poor, tired feet from their shoes had him surging past the others. He couldn't wait for some shut-eye, and if the wagging tail on Defender was any indication, his dog looked forward to it, too.

On the other side of the threshold a walled clearing expanded outward and upward to an oval opening high above their heads. The enclosed space should've been overcast and gloomy, but golden light seemed to be infused like heavy cream in the fire-scented air.

Moss, lichen, and vines coated many rocky surfaces in various greens, yellows, and grays. Berry bushes beckoned the weary travelers, their heavy branches laden with ripening fruits. Christoffer plucked a few and ate them as they crossed the clearing, enjoying their juicy flesh.

Thick, swaying grasses formed a carpet path to the base of a single, oversized tree, an ancient oak, home to the witch of the woods. Being October, most of its leaves were various oranges and reds with a few yellows and browns tucked between, like precious notes from a loved one. Leaves from the outer edges had already begun to fall from brushing into the walls surrounding the glen.

Smoke tendrils drifted out of a small chimney cleverly nestled in one of the tree's heavy limbs. The mouthwatering scent of something cooking had Christoffer's eyes glazing and made him think of all the comforts and delights of fall. Defender sniffed curiously at the air and whined.

"Steady," Christoffer murmured to him as they approached the giant oak.

Floral patterned rosemåling spiraled around its trunk to stop at a faded Dutch-style door in the center of the tree. Christoffer registered only mild surprise that its repainting hadn't been one of the Stag Lord's duties during his summers with the witch. Old paint, bleached out in odd striations, curled and buckled as it warped away from the door. It added a feeling of home and hearth to a place that was as whimsical as it was foreign.

Totally at ease, Henrik bounded up the step and rapped on the door with his knuckles, the antlers on his cloak scraping against the frame. The upper portion of the door opened revealing a spry old woman with silver-blonde hair peeking out from under a solid cobalt scarf. She wore a patched matching apron, and in her hands she cupped a ladle filled with a warm burnt-orange colored liquid.

"Stag Lord try this," she demanded upon seeing him and thrust the ladle under his nose.

He sucked in a mouthful of the broth and hummed his approval. "That is good, witch."

"You don't think it's missing something? I'm teaching a young brownie how to make pumpkin soup, and I could swear it's missing something."

"You have a brownie?" Filip asked, peering inside.

"Not yet. I have many applicants, of course, more so now, since King Aleks freed them from Niffleheim, but I will only accept the best of the best to be my brownie."

Aleks ran a hand through his hair, exposing his ears. He said, "I take it this one doesn't yet have his Master or her Madam?"

"Train them while they're young," the witch said, smacking at the soup. "Aha! I have it. The soup needs more mace, cloves, and salt, Magga."

"Magga?" Geirr asked. "Who's Magga?"

"Why, the brownie," answered the witch, looking at him with concern. "You look tired. Have you been walking all night?"

"We have," said Henrik, answering not only for Geirr, but for them all.

His friend, whose eyebrows had shot up to his hairline, interjected, "She has a name?"

The witch chortled. "Of course, boy, brownies have names, but they gladly forfeit them for their titles. A Madam or Master, after all, is their highest honor."

Henrik leaned against the Dutch sill, which placed half his antlers inside her home. The sight had her *tsking* and she swatted at him. His grin was unrepentant.

"Like the witch," he explained, "brownies believe names have power. In this way the collective names represent strength, respect, and ability, while also being a shield against dragons and their corrupting influences."

Christoffer raised a hand. "Then how come we know Magga's name at all?"

The witch eyed him speculatively. "Who says it is her real name? Only she knows it. What she chooses to be called is irrelevant."

Filip's brow furrowed at that. "Wouldn't at least her parents know her name? After all they gave it to her."

"Is the name given at birth the real name or a label? Doesn't the soul know its true name?"

"Wait, wait, wait. If that's the case, why do you have us call you witch?" asked Aleks, ignoring Filip's question. "Why aren't you Martha, or Mary, or – or – something?"

"I'm calling shenanigans," Christoffer said, eyes twinkling.

When the witch grinned, her face wrinkled in mischievousness as her snaggle tooth flashed. "I am but a humble witch, not important enough in the grand scheme of things to be called by name."

Henrik scoffed. "You don't deceive us."

She laughed, and it was more like a cackle, raising the hairs on Christoffer's neck. Swinging open the bottom half of her door and pointing with the ladle, she beckoned them inside. "Step into my home, and why don't you tell me what brought you for this unexpected and out of season visit. Leave the dog outside."

"I wonder if news of your time at Olaf's home got around, old fellow. Behave," muttered Christoffer, scratching Defender's ears. He yawned, cracking his jaw in the process, and crossed over the threshold.

As he entered the witch's home behind Geirr and Zaria, the first thing that jumped out at him, was its roundish and odd dimensions. It felt much like a mountain-troll's home inside a stalagmite. Where the stalagmite felt rough and cold, however, the witch's tree home welcomed with a warm fire in a stone hearth, filling the room to bursting with the delicious aroma that he soon hoped to call his lunch.

Mimicking a mountain-troll's home, the witch had an unobstructed floor plan taken up by a singular room. He did not spy a sink, and presumed it must be outside somewhere behind her home. To the right of him, a wall of pantry doors hid a slew of basic food stuffs. A step stool stood nearby to assist the brownie and witch in reaching the upper shelves.

Over their heads, strings – taut and crowded with rich and earthy ingredients – ran from wall to wall, crisscrossing and looping in ways that boggled the mind. All the items were in various stages of drying, from freshly picked and raw, to dark and dehydrated.

Discarded, a broom lay on its side by the back wall. Next to it, a small narrow ladder led to an upstairs room. Christoffer craned his neck, but could not see anything other than the edge of a white and blue quilt. It must be the witch's bedroom.

Straightening, he looked to the left. Studying them, Magga wiped down a freestanding countertop with the end of her apron. Heat spilling from the hearth behind where she stood, turned her blue cheeks a warm purple color. Her eyes narrowed in dislike the instant she felt his stare. He wondered absently what her deal was, but dismissed the thought.

A large black pot holding the rest of the orange liquid Henrik had tasted, hung above the crackling fire. The aroma called to Christoffer, and he gravitated toward it, reaching for the ladle. Magga slapped the back of his hand with her wooden spoon, like he was a naughty child. Smarting, he pressed his mouth to it and glared, his gaze narrowing as he watched her give Aleks a sample as soon as he came over.

Magga grinned smugly at him, unseen by the others. He decided he didn't like the brownie one bit; she ranked right down there with the cantankerous Master Brown living under Álfheim. In fact, the more Christoffer thought about it, the more he was inclined to rank Master Brown favorably, for what the brownie lacked in personality, he made up for in ability and location, making him worthy of his title. The underground water wheel he commanded was everything magical. His job as gatekeeper between the elf and mountain-troll realms was cool, too.

"Can Magga get any of you something to drink? You must be parched."

"I could have something," Zaria said, letting Filip take her coat. She brushed at the fly-aways around her face, pushing them back.

"Same," Henrik said, hanging his cloak on a peg along the wall.

He pulled out a stool from behind the counter and sat down, settling onto his elbows. He plucked a berry from the bowl beside the brownie. Zaria did the same, bringing it to her lips with a happy sigh. Christoffer noted Magga didn't swat at their hands either.

Was it him or humans in general she didn't like? As if reading his thoughts, she skewered him with a glare daring him to try to do the same. Ah, so it was him.

For whatever reason, she definitely didn't like him. The feeling was mutual.

The witch snapped her towel playfully at the Stag Lord's backside. She teased, "Look at this one, Magga, making himself at home."

"One might think he missed us," Magga replied, a faint smile on her thin lips.

Henrik stayed quiet, but a smile played about his mouth. He stole another handful of berries, turning to offer them to Zaria. She declined with a wave of her hand and sat down on the only other stool. Filip leaned around her and swiped a berry before Magga could stop him. She was, however, ready for Christoffer when he attempted once more.

"Curse you," he grumbled under his breath.

"Berry thief," she hissed back.

Stung, he returned, "I am no thief."

"I saw you outside," she murmured.

"Outside?"

"Yes outside. All things in the glen belong to the witch. You stole from her. Thief."

Unhearing, the witch stirred the soup and tasted it again. "Hmm. This is exactly right. Stag Lord, fetch the bowls. You know where they are."

"Yes, witch," he said, standing and going back to the wall of cabinets.

Christoffer stole his seat and deliberately grabbed a large handful of berries when the brownie turned to gather a teapot and a pitcher. On return she glared at him, and he stuck out his tongue. She sneered for a second, careful to keep it from the witch.

"I'll grab the cups, if you tell me where they're located," offered Geirr.

The brownie smiled graciously at him and Christoffer didn't trust it for a minute. She pointed to a cupboard, and Geirr ambled off to get them, returning a moment later. The witch had already begun filling bowls with steaming hot soup. She asked Zaria to create a few ice cubes to place in them so they wouldn't burn anyone on ingestion.

Magga plunked a cup in front of Christoffer splashing him with a cool liquid. "Here you go, young sir."

"Thanks," he said, wishing he'd paid attention to see if she'd spat in it. He wouldn't put it past her.

After everyone was settled, with most standing and crowding around her counter, the witch leaned back and measured them with her gaze. Christoffer dropped his to look at the soup as he took a cautious sip. Pumpkin, and perfectly creamy with a hint of citrus, possibly lime.

"Ask me," the witch said at last, levelling Henrik with a look.

He swallowed and nodded. "We're not able to give you details, but we're in need of assistance."

"Don't you trust me, Stag Lord? How can I help without details?"

Zaria wiped her mouth. "It's not that. I wish I could say more. I'm sorry."

"A mysterious visit cloaked in enigmatic phrases. You must be out on a task relating to dragons. And you're here because you were what – not provided instructions?" she postulated, thinking aloud.

Christoffer was impressed by how fast she reasoned that one out. All around her kitchen, his friends stared askance at one another. He took another spoonful of soup and waited to see what would happen next. Nobody rushed to confirm or deny it, which probably confirmed it for the witch.

When she said nothing, Aleks baldly asked, "Can you help?"

"Perhaps, drink your tea."

"I have water," grumbled Christoffer.

"Drink your water," Magga snapped, keeping her voice low.

"Are you going to read tea leaves?" asked Christoffer, ignoring the brownie.

"Don't be silly," said the witch. "What can leaves say? Have they mouths? Are they intelligent?"

Taken aback he said, "But, isn't that what witches do? Isn't that what you did before when predicting Aleks' future? What do you do with all these herbs?"

"Cook," replied Magga, as if it were obvious.

"Then how did you make the golden shoes?" Christoffer questioned. He waved about the ceiling, "Did you not use all of this?"

"Trade secrets," the witch said, with a feline smile.

Frustrated with the witch's answers, he frowned at the others. Zaria shrugged and nudged him with her shoulder. She nodded toward her bag, gently reminding him they were being equally mysterious. He sighed in acknowledgement and went back to eating. He hated being thwarted when he tried to learn how magic worked. Even if he couldn't wield it, he still thirsted to know everything about it.

Not for the first time he wondered why Queen Helena set them on the impossible task of replacing the Drakeland Sword. Why keep its destruction quiet? Okay, so he understood that one – the dragons would find out, or Floki, or someone, and that would ultimately bring the news to the dragons. Of all the measures in the Under Realm that kept them in check, they feared the sword, because it could best them.

So why not tell them exactly whom they needed to find? Or where they needed to go to complete the quest? Video game quests never felt this challenging. There was a clear path, a destination, a series of events and sub-tasks that led one to the ultimate goal. Here in the middle of the witch's glen in Gloomwood Forest there were none of those things.

Henrik finished his soup and wiped his mouth with his hand. "That was delicious. Witch, have you decided if you would help us?"

She tapped her chin and set down her spoon with deliberate care. "I will help in exchange for something in return."

The look on the Stag Lord's face turned anticipatory, and the negotiations began. He rubbed his hands together and leaned forward. "Excellent, excellent. What is your price?"

Staring at him shrewdly she placed her hands on the table. "With dragons involved, surely I could not be expected to help without recompense equal to the task at hand. Why don't you tell me something first, so I can accurately calculate my fee."

He shook his head. "You know far too much already, witch, to be given more. Name your price."

She glowered at him. "I shall take nothing less than the right to name your son, and he shall reside here in my glen for the time he is Hart."

"You must be joking," said Henrik, settling back on his stool and folding his arms. "That is not a favor I can grant."

"You can."

"I can't," he stated firmly. "Harts always grow up amongst their grandfathers in the center of the Golden Kings. Harts choose their names, and my son will be no different.

"And besides heritage and tradition, as you have said, names are power. Why would I give you that in exchange for a wee bit of assistance that will neither tax you or cause you to leave the comfort of your own home?"

Her face fell a fraction, but she rallied and counteroffered. "If you can't give me that small thing, then give me a princeling's ransom and extend your stay with me for three more summers."

"Worse and worse," the Stag Lord said. "You ask for too great a price. Try asking me for a hulder's tail or a maiden's first kiss, now those I could do for you easily."

"No, no, no. Now you are belittling my assistance. I am not sought out for just any old help. I am sought by individuals like Queen Helena, your father, King Flein, King Aleks' family, and Petronella the Measureless. Rulers seek me out for things they just can't get any old place or from any old person. I will take your first kiss, Stag Lord, not some maiden's. Yours is more valuable."

His brown-haired friend grimaced and avoided looking anyone in the eye. Of their own volition, Christoffer's eyebrows raised. Hadn't Henrik been his wingman many times? Had they not escorted some very pretty girls to the movies and around the parks? Yet, how had he not had his first kiss? Surely the witch was wrong. He couldn't be saving it. Not for Zaria; she wasn't available.

"How about I bring you a travel mirror from Jerndor, set in a frame by the Stabbursdalen giants? Or a bottle stoppered with a mare's terror?" Henrik haggled.

"I have no vanity," she said toothily. "Nor need I a good night's sleep. What else do you offer?"

Aleks fingered his bag and nodding to himself brought it onto the counter. He fished inside for something and pulled out an empty sack. "I can give you this," he said, laying it out for inspection.

She seized it eagerly and studied it, nose first. "A dwarfish sack of holding, very nice. What's inside I wonder? Ah, weapons. I might have guessed. Do you see this magical stitching? It will never pull."

"Will you take it?" Aleks asked.

"No, little Raven King," she said, passing it back.

"No?" Aleks questioned, frowning.

"You will need it more, I think." She scratched her chin and looked between the group, settling her glimmering gaze upon Filip. "Aha! I have it. You will bring me back the first two items you collect from the sea. That is my fee."

Henrik smiled and folded his hands. "I will bring you back the first —"

"This is nonnegotiable. I am decided," said the witch. "What will be it, Stag Lord?"

He caught Zaria's gaze. Softly he said, "Princess?"

"Two unnamed items?" she asked the witch.

"Like a seashell and a pebble?" Filip clarified, resting a hand on the sorceress' shoulder.

"What will you do with that? Decorate your cat's collar?" Christoffer felt horribly disappointed with the request. Where was the adventure in bringing back a seashell or a pebble?

The witch cackled. "I have no cat."

"Oh, we're out. No deal. Never trust a witch without a cat," swore Christoffer, flabbergasting the group.

Magga looked ready to skewer him on her mistress' behalf. She fumed, "You have no respect."

"Christoffer," Zaria warned.

"You know I'm right. When has there ever been a witch without a cat? It's suspicious."

The witch clucked her tongue. "I do not want what is common from the sea. You will know what I want, when you come across it."

"It's a deal," said Henrik, extending his hand. "Providing your assistance is –"

She waggled a finger at him. "Tut. Tut. No provisos, alterations, deviations, or caveats, Stag Lord. Haven't you been reading your father's journals? You know better."

He flexed his fingers. "Deal."

She spat in her hand and grabbed his firmly, pumping once. "Good boy. Help Magga, would you, to tidy up, while I go and get what you need."

When the witch returned, the dishes had been washed in a trough behind her treehouse, her downstairs swept, and food prepped and stored for future use. Magga had done very little, mostly supervising, taking great pleasure in directing Christoffer. He wanted to feed her to Defender for lunch, but was afraid to give his dog indigestion. All this over a few berries plucked and eaten. The brownie had not a single hospitable bone in her body to begrudge him that.

With a great deal of gravity, she said, "That which you seek can only be gained by fulfilling the promises you've already made."

"What do you mean?" Henrik asked, eyes narrowing.

"Just what I said," the witch replied, holding a bundle to her chest. "You have made promises that others took on good faith. Something is undone you must do. If you figure it out, you will be rewarded."

Zaria shook her head, rubbing her temples. "That's it? That's all the help you're going to give? What promise hasn't been kept?"

"How should I know, Princess? I wasn't there when you and your friends made the promise." The witch handed her the bundle. "This will help you, too, but don't unwrap it until you are in need of something."

"As in something besides answers, I suppose," Geirr muttered in frustration. "That would be too easy."

"It's the ravens," said Christoffer suddenly, having cast his thoughts backwards searching for the broken promise. His brown-eyed gaze bounced between the others who watched him with various expressions of understanding. To Henrik, he asked, "Have you brought Master Brown his white ravens?"

# Chapter Six: Ever Elleken

"I have not," Henrik said, groaning. "You don't think he's forgotten have you?"

"No," everyone said at once, remembering the tetchy brownie.

Nodding in acceptance he said, "Witch, do you have six white ravens?"

Her cackle turned into a dry heaving hiss of pure amusement. Wheezing, she said, "I do not. That is a prince's ransom."

"Tell me about it," the Stag Lord rumbled.

They rested the remainder of the afternoon and evening, puzzling out their next move and sleeping where they could find space in the witch's home.

Christoffer didn't have the best sleep, because he kept feeling the brownie's gaze on him. He'd wake sometimes to find her staring so hard he was surprised there wasn't a hole from her laser-beamed scowl. She was like his own personal mare, making his sleep fretful. He was glad when the others finally began stirring the next morning.

As they finished their breakfast, Henrik swept the group with his deep-blue gaze and announced, "We must go to Jötunheim to find the raven without a master."

"One talking raven," Zaria said thoughtfully, looking up at the herbs above her head as if the raven was already there.

"Will it be easier to convince this raven to go to Master Brown than to find six non-talking ones?" asked Filip.

"I think so, yes," said Henrik.

Annoyed, Geirr folded his arms across his muscular chest. "Are you telling me that we could have delayed the start of our trip and hitched a ride with Olaf and Bjarke? Wonderful."

Filip clapped him on his shoulder, maneuvering him out the witch's door, allowing the others to take their leave of the witch and her hospitality. "Ease up, mate.

Don't be so tense. We're not in school. That counts for something."

"I had a date," Geirr complained, striding away from the tree trunk and alerting Defender who sat up and watched with curiosity.

"Wait, you had a date and didn't invite me? What gives?" Christoffer counter-complained, jogging to catch up. His actions drew a woof and a trot from the border collie. "Wingman, bro. Come on!"

"Wingman doesn't mean what you think it means," Geirr said, rolling his eyes. "I already had the date. I didn't need a wingman."

"Not the point, man," he pouted. "I could have invited Kirsi from third period. Double date."

"I didn't want you distracting Sofie, all right," Geirr said a little heatedly. "You hog all the attention."

"I do not."

"You do. Or don't you remember what happened with Mille?"

"That wasn't my fault!"

Defender barked in agreement, looking up at him with absolute adoration. Christoffer appreciated the moral support, as Filip came up along his other side. The blond teen had grown into his tall frame and easily outpaced them both, spinning around to jog backwards, grinning.

"It was," said Filip. "You're lucky Geirr didn't punch you in the nose."

Defensive, he said, "If he had been livelier, it wouldn't have happened."

"Missing the point," Geirr said, narrowing his gaze.

"Do you think we could cut across the forest and still hitch that ride?" Zaria asked, showing up at the edge of the glen with Aleks and Henrik in tow. At first, Christoffer was confused, still wholly focused on his argument with Geirr, but seeing her pointed look at Aleks and Henrik, the group's navigator and local guide respectively, he cottoned on, especially when she added, "You know, with Bjarke and Olaf?"

"We could head south to Trondheim," offered Aleks, indicating the general direction.

Henrik countered, pointing north. "We could go to the Elleken camp."

"Ooo, I vote north," said Christoffer, feeling like a kid in a candy store.

In all their travels, none of them had seen the home of the ellefolken. Hector had taken them to Álfheim, which was close, and their peoples were like cousins to each other with much intermarrying, but not to

Elleken. From what Henrik had revealed it was like an elaborate roving campsite. In his mind it seemed like it might belong in look and feel to the Sami peoples – close-knit, colorful, and cheerful. He was already excited to see it.

"I would love to see your home," Zaria said, her hand in Filip's.

He gave it a squeeze and nodded, hooking his free thumb in his back pocket. It seemed to Christoffer with that gesture and easy agreement to go to the Stag Lord's kingdom that Filip felt more confident in his relationship with Zaria than ever before, and no longer worried about Henrik's unrequited interest.

"Very well," said Aleks acquiescing and motioning to Henrik to lead the way.

The Stag Lord led the others through the woods toward his home, occasionally lifting the heart-slash-arrow-like shaped pendant around his neck into the light. When Christoffer asked what he was doing, Henrik explained that the pendant focused light to direct him home, which he thought an interesting turn of phrase because the pendant, in the hands of Hector, his father, had found Henrik, when he was Hart.

Is that how it worked for Hector? Was Henrik his home? Perhaps, home wasn't a place like Elleken, but a person who lived there. But if it were a person and not a place, then the pendant would've led Henrik to a different place than Elleken by now, wouldn't it?

Perhaps not. Most of the ellefolken only ever lived in and around Elleken. He had only met a few outside of their kingdom, and they were all on Bjarke's vessel. Maybe, if it were a person, then this person was the very someone the Stag Lord would fall in love with, marry, and someday bring into the world the next little Hart. It was a thought he kept to himself... at least for now. He'd sit back and observe and see if his suspicions were true.

If they were true, then Christoffer had even more questions. Why hadn't anyone told Henrik? Why hadn't Hector, either in his journals or conversations, mentioned whether the magical properties of the pendant drew him to Henrik's mother? Or why hadn't Hakon, his grandfather, or any of the previous kings who schooled him amongst the Golden Kings? Or did they not know themselves? And if they didn't know themselves, did that mean that Christoffer's theory was completely bogus?

The more complicated and even more farfetched the matter became, the more he dwelled on it, so Christoffer pulled himself back to the present, leaving his postulations behind. Noticing Defender tracking something through the grasses, Christoffer called for him to leave it, but the small animal – a rabbit –

began running, and there was no hope of stopping him.

As the border collie chased after the rabbit, so too, did he chase after Defender. Calling for help, Aleks and Filip joined him on the mad dash through the trees. Even with all three in pursuit, Defender led them on a merry game of keep away, even after losing the rabbit to its burrow, only coming close when each was clearly too exhausted to even lunge for the dog.

They picked their way over logs and through small streams, hopping across where they could, and wading where they couldn't, slowing them down. The slope of the land shifted underfoot like a sleeping giant's even breaths. The little hills and valleys served to tire them out even more, but not Defender. He wore a loony grin like the game was still afoot.

"You win," Filip told the dog, giving up and trotting back to Zaria, where she wiped away a lock of sweaty hair that had fallen into his green eyes.

She gave him a quick kiss on the mouth and danced away, laughing at his exaggerated moue of disappointment. "You're a little ripe."

"All the better to hug you then," he growled, and sprang after her.

She shrieked and ran off and soon another chase was in play, one which Defender tried to join, but was decidedly left out. They disappeared into the woods finding new energy in their flirting. Occasional flashes of color revealed their location, but it was the hum of their joy and an excited woof which let everyone know they were nearby. Christoffer leaned over, hands upon his knees, and gulped down air, as Aleks stopped beside him.

"I think he wore us out more than we wore him out," Aleks commented drily, when he had breath.

Christoffer laughed weakly. "That's Defender, all right. He might not need it, but I'm ready for a nap. How long before we're there?"

Frowning, he glanced upwards through the trees at the misty light filtering down from the sky. "Perhaps a few more hours, but that's only if Elleken is located where I think it is."

"You're back to normal on your navigational know-how so you're probably right. Carry me?"

Smirking, Aleks shook his head. "Come on, lazy bones, we got some more walking to do."

He groaned, but straightened up and followed his friend, rejoining Henrik and Geirr. The afternoon passed by in a happy blur with Zaria and Filip finding their way back about twenty minutes after Defender decided to return to the group. From Filip's grin and Zaria's becoming blush Christoffer guessed that one of them caught the other and took a few moments to themselves. He nudged Geirr knowingly which prompted an eyeroll in response.

Zaria passed around snacks for everyone — sweet juicy fruit, warm fragrant breads, and sharp tasty cheeses. Christoffer licked a rivulet of pear juice from his arm and flicked the core into the trees. He conned her into chocolate chip cookies next, wheedling until she capitulated, which he knew she didn't mind; those were her favorite dessert.

As the day entwined itself in the robes of twilight, a soft cool rain began to fall. Defender splashed through puddles and kicked up mud, happy as a bear in a camper's rubbish bin. Between one breath and the next they arrived at Elleken. The very trees seemed to part of their own volition — perhaps they were ellefolken themselves — before giving way to a browning meadow space.

"Pinch me," said Christoffer, unprepared for the sights before him. Geirr obliged, and he yelped. "I didn't mean it, man."

"I only did what you asked. Next time be more specific," said Geirr, unrepentant. Rain pearled like dew in his hair and dripped steadily from his charcoal-colored eyebrows.

Christoffer and the others were much the same, thoroughly soaked, but bearing well under it. He rubbed his arm distractedly, looking around in awe at the incredible thriving hub of the ellefolken's nomadic home. He could hardly take it all in.

The rain detracted not a whit from its inherent beauty. It made everything glisten as it sprinkled, appearing not to fall, but to form on surfaces like diamonds and pieces of glass. Everywhere fat globular drops shimmered and sighed, refusing to slide to earth, defying gravity.

Flickering shadows and firelight glowed from within canvas and leather-lined tents that sprawled across both sides of the Gjöll, narrower here than Christoffer had ever seen. Abandoned canoes lined both banks, ready for quick sailings back and forth for visits with friends. The magical river danced and shivered like the sounds of musical notes, a visible rendering of the rain's song.

The air itself wavered as if magic thickened it, giving it weight and substance. Or maybe it was the incredible aroma of spices and cooking meats causing his stomach to gurgle. Fires in bronze braziers hissed and spit within the tent's openings, joining in the river's dancing, and revealing their occupants.

Ellefolken women and girls worked at various tasks. All around they could be seen and heard talking, cooking, sewing, beading, braiding, carving, cleaning, eating, drinking, reading, laughing, caretaking, washing, playing, and singing. All the happy activity brought him to a standstill. He could not take his eyes off them.

Most wore muted clothing in grays, creams, and browns. Some wore pine green or navy, but almost all wore their elk pelt on their person like Henrik did his. Where the Stag Lord's pelt was white as a snowdrift, the women's were dark brown like the earthen floor beneath his feet. Some fashioned their pelts as dresses with beaded belts, some as skirts with embroidery, some as cloaks like Henrik, some as ponchos, and some as tunics with beaded trim or as plain sturdy work pants.

Elk – the ellefolken in an alternate form – and reindeer luxuriated happily under tender ministrations, enjoying being groomed or petted. Muscular flanks were brushed, ears rubbed, noses scratched, hoofs trimmed, and fur combed.

One and all they seemed so blissfully content Christoffer hesitated to come closer to their hidden paradise for fear of disturbing it. Henrik, however, had no such compunction and strode into the nearest tent calling out for his mother and aunts, at once both an interloper and a most desired missing member to the scene. His strong, steady presence practically compelled the attention of the females. A cry went up in greeting, as his call for family spread out to the nearby tents until they'd been found.

A small, older woman ran into the tent, her dark mahogany hair and shoulders dewed with rain. She ran to Henrik and swept him into her fierce embrace. He stooped and enfolded her as well. Her mouth curved into a wide smile, and she laughingly called out for a feast to be prepared for her prodigal son's return. She straightened his antlered cloak around his shoulders and patted him on the chest.

"Everyone, come meet my mother," Henrik invited, drawing them closer.

Zaria reached out to be the first to clasp her hands. "I've heard so much about you," she said. "It's so nice to meet you at last."

"Princess Zaria," she said, casting her son a knowing look, which he tried his best to ignore. "You are just as pretty as Henrik described. Prettier even."

Henrik groaned, "She's lying."

"I am, am I?" the ellefolken queen murmured, raising an eyebrow, causing Christoffer to snicker.

Henrik threw him a pleading look, and he shrugged back. What else was he supposed to do? The guy was hopelessly infatuated with Zaria and had been for years. He would have to suffer his mother's embarrassing proclamations.

"Yes, you are," Henrik insisted, looking as uncomfortable as Zaria now appeared to be.

"Thank you, Queen Wenche," Zaria said with an awkward laugh, before inclining her head graciously and stepping away.

"How did you know her name? Henrik's only ever called her mum," Filip said, looking between the three of them curiously.

"From Hector's journals," she said.

"That explains it," he murmured, nodding. "I remember you devouring those when Henrik first loaned them."

"I missed him," she said softly. "I still do."

Henrik's mother smiled softly at her. "He is not lost to us, dear one."

The Stag Lord squeezed her shoulder. "It's just a little harder to talk to him is all."

Gathering her son under her arm, Wenche gestured to the hexagonal tent. "Come in and warm yourselves by the fire. Trade your wet clothes for furs and pelts and soft woven cloths. We have plenty to spare. We are so pleased to have you with us."

"Even Defender?" asked Christoffer, holding back his eager dog.

"Even him," agreed Wenche.

"Your bad manners haven't made it this far north," teased Christoffer. "Don't go getting into trouble."

"He was pretty bad at Olaf's, wasn't he?" Zaria giggled.

"He was a terror," affirmed Christoffer.

"Olaf's? Then he deserved it, and worse, whatever your dog did," said Henrik's mother, taking in the border collie's lolling tongue and eager gaze with new pleasure.

"I'm home now," Henrik said, squeezing her tight.

She hugged him back. "I am thankful for that. No more dwelling on bad memories. Let us celebrate your return."

With sighs of relief and gratitude, backpacks were tossed into a pile beside a deep nest of throws and cushions. Christoffer eagerly began shedding his damp and chaffing clothes, starting with his shirt. It got stuck halfway up around his shoulders. Grunting for help, he thanked the unseen person who freed him.

When the shirt disappeared, his eyes collided with a beautiful blonde with soft cloudy curls, wide indigo eyes, and rosy cheeks. Short antlers about a foot high sprung from the crown of her head, and when she smiled his heart beat faster than a hummingbird's wings. He couldn't find his tongue and blinked stupidly at her.

"Hello," she said. "I'm Pia."

"Christoffer. I like your antlers," he blurted.

Her smile broadened as she fingered the leaf carvings etched in one. "It's scrimshaw," she explained at his admiring look. "My cousin is the artist."

"Does it act like a tattoo?" he asked. "Is it permanent? I mean of course it's permanent, but can you – I don't know – sand it off and start again if you wanted to change it?"

She shook her head. "It's more like a tattoo."

Pia led him to a roped off section of the large tent. Blankets hung over the ropes providing a private changing space. Inside he found a pair of brown pants and a long-sleeve navy shirt. He shucked his wet denim and underthings and put on the offerings, feeling them settle warmly over his chilled skin.

When he emerged, Pia took his wet things and gestured to where his friends sat warming themselves by the fire. Defender was on his back, tail wagging and tongue lolling, as two young ellefolken girls scratched his belly and cooed over him, feeding him little handfuls of chicken.

As Christoffer walked over, a trio of teenage girls came from another tent with heavily laden trays heaped with fruits, breads, cheeses, meats, and drinks. Henrik and Filip stood up to help place them on the low tables. The two carrying the trays Henrik took tittered and blushed with the third as they fawned over the Stag Lord, ignoring his human friend.

Henrik had shed his golden antlered cloak and changed into all white – even the hems were embroidered in white. With his bronzed skin and well-defined muscles, he looked every inch a prince. At this point, Christoffer didn't think his friend needed a wingman, so much as a willingness to play the field.

"You're like prime meat to these girls," he said to Henrik, taking a seat next to him as the trio left whispering and giggling.

Henrik looked up, frowning at their retreating figures. "They don't even know me."

"They would if you didn't spend all your time with us in Fredrikstad going to school and hanging out with the witch of the woods," Christoffer countered.

"I like school and the witch isn't so bad," Henrik murmured, handing him a small, well-made kuksa filled with warm pine-bark tea.

"You don't have to date them, but you should get to know some of them. Pia is nice."

"You sound like my mother," Henrik complained. "You've been here all of five minutes. How do you know one of these girls to recommend her?"

"She helped me get changed and I asked her name."

"Did you know my mother returned from tree form to ensure I found a girl? Apparently she, my aunts, and my grandfather are worried that I won't produce an heir. I don't understand what the rush is."

"Not your father, though?" Christoffer asked, picking up a scrimshawed antler-handled knife with an elk illustration and cutting into the cheese plate.

"He understands," Henrik said, plucking up a ripe plum and biting into its flesh. "He explained how he knew my mother was the one. I'm waiting for that same recognition."

"Oh, so it does get explained," Christoffer said, feeling dumb about his previous conjectures. "Is it like magic?" And then, unable to help himself, "Does it have to do with your necklace?"

Henrik fingered the pendant. "No, it does not. What a notion." He sighed. "I find I like your explanation better. That would make everything easier."

"So, how do you know when you find her?"

"My father said it feels like finding sunshine. My grandfather says it's more like getting concussed just at the sight of her."

"Of the two, I think I'd prefer the sunshine. And, do you think you found sunshine or a concussion in Zaria?" Christoffer asked skeptically.

Henrik sighed again and looked toward the fire. "I like her, but I'm not stupid. She's dating Filip. I won't get in the way of that. They're both my friends."

Christoffer drained his cup and leaned over to refill it. "You still want to date her. You even told your mother she was pretty."

Henrik groaned and raked a hand through his tussled hair. "I don't think she's 'the one' or that we're star-crossed lovers or whatever."

"But you're still hoping they might break up and you'd get a shot. You shouldn't be wishing that."

"I'm not," Henrik insisted, though his eyes strayed across the fire to where Zaria and Filip cuddled side by side eating grapes and sharing a roasted rabbit.

Christoffer let it slide, knowing his friend needed more time to mourn what couldn't be. Sometimes destiny and responsibilities sucked. He was glad they wouldn't fall on his shoulders. Settling in for the opulent meal, he relaxed and talked with his friend about life, ravens, and the future.

Cool breezes blew through the tent's openings as visitors came in and sought audience with the Stag Lord. Petty squabbles were resolved, flirtatious overtures were made and ignored, little gifts and tributes left behind, and news shared. Henrik was good at his job, ruling with fairness and ease in a way Christoffer didn't think he could ever pull off and once more was glad he didn't have to try. He wondered if Aleks felt as comfortable in his role over the fey.

When the evening drew to a close, the rain had stopped, and the temperatures dropped. Wenche returned with two women, who turned out to be Henrik's aunts, and escorted them to their sleeping tents. Henrik went off with his mother alone, while Defender stayed back at the main tent snoring beside the fire. Christoffer followed behind Geirr and Aleks and the two aunts, with Zaria and Filip behind him. Barely able to shuffle his feet forward as full and relaxed as he was, Christoffer looked forward to sleeping in a nice warm bed.

A sharp cry rent the air, startling him awake. He looked overhead searching the night sky for the source and found it in the pale ghostly form gliding through the trees.

"Eye-riii!" Airi shouted again in triumph as she wheeled around, landing on her master.

"Hello my clever girl," Aleks said delightedly. "I wasn't expecting to see you so soon. Did you miss me or do you have a message for me?"

"Nori says, 'Hags chased out of plains.'"

"That's good," said Aleks. "I knew Sivert could do it. Anything from Saskia?" She held out her ankle and Aleks took the message tied around it. "Why don't you go grab something to eat from the main tent and find a place to rest. You must be tired. I will give you messages to return with in the morning."

Christoffer yawned and rubbed his eyes. "Why can't you just text like normal people?"

"Jealous, are we? Or are you missing your beauty sleep already? I don't think it's going to help you much," Aleks teased back.

"You're one to talk, I don't think you could get any uglier," Geirr mocked, ducking into the tent. "What is this about hags, though?"

"We almost lost a Spring child to one of the invading packs before we even realized they were down in the plains. I told Sivert to handle the infestation promptly before they became entrenched. I don't want them or their wolverines eating unsuspecting fey."

"You should have said something earlier," Zaria said. "You don't think it's dragon related do you?"

"Not everything is," Aleks replied, his brow furrowing in thought. "Still, no, I don't think so. I think some hags saw an opportunity with the new openings between Norway and Niffleheim and tried to nest in the plains."

"Let's hope that's true," said Filip, claiming a spot on one of the piles of fur pelts. "The last thing we need is a dragon at work among the disenfranchised factions of Norway."

"Amen to that," agreed Christoffer, sinking down into another pile of pelts and closing his eyes with a deep sigh.

"I take offense. I'm trying to eliminate feelings of disenfranchisement," huffed Aleks, but Christoffer was already heading toward oblivion and made no comment.

"Not the fey, oh Raven King," Filip replied, yawning. "The hags."

"Oh," he said, mollified.

Defender appeared with a tired woof and found a spot next to Christoffer. His warm presence a source of loyal comfort, boy and dog slumbered as one, knowing they were both loved and protected.

# Chapter Seven: An Evasive Maneuver

The next day dawned gray and chilly as the wind breathed wetly against their skin, raising gooseflesh. Christoffer debated putting on his warmer underclothes and decided to be prudent rather than sorry. After all, what were layers for, if one didn't wear and shed them as needed?

As Defender went off into the nearby trees to do his business, he made his way with Zaria to the main tent. Geirr was still getting ready, and Filip was still sleeping, minus his habitual snoring. Christoffer had been surprised and looked questioningly at her, but Zaria smiled impishly and waggled her fingers.

"The miracles of magic?" he asked, grinning.

Zaria nodded, and explained, "He only snores on his back, so I created a blanket barrier keeping him on his side and voila! A goodnight's sleep for all."

"Why Zaria," he teased. "How do you know Filip only snores on his back?"

"Oh hush," she scolded, grabbing his arm just above his elbow and dragging him along. "Get your mind out of the gutter, would you?"

"Hey, you brought it up, Princess," he said, raising his hands in surrender.

"We've fallen asleep on date nights at his house –"

"Uh-huh, sure, sure," he agreed, smirking.

"On the couch," she insisted, glaring.

His eyes twinkled, as he suppressed a chuckle. "I'm not knocking where you decide to do the deed."

"We were watching movies into the early morning," she defended, tilting her chin stubbornly.

"There's a phrase for that," he baited, but when her fingers sparked purple, he twisted out of reach and danced merrily away. "Okay! Okay! Whatever you say. I believe you."

"You'd better," she growled before relenting and dropping her scary stance.

He dropped his guard, and she nailed him with a purple stinger. "Ouch!" he complained, rubbing his backside.

"You deserved it," she informed him haughtily, before grabbing his arm again and hauling him into the community tent.

There they found Henrik looking harried, sitting on a low pile of furs and pillows surrounded by females. Most of them were older – his mother and aunts, but a few were their age and clearly throwing out lures to catch a Stag Lord. His focus on his family and politics kept him from noticing. Upon seeing them he waved them over and pushed the younger girls back to make room. They eyed Zaria with jealousy, as she accepted a spot next to him.

Henrik buttered a piece of toast and slathered jam on it, which Christoffer intercepted before he could hand it to her. Not because it was wrong for Henrik to give her the toast, but because Christoffer didn't think Henrik realized how upset the females around him were at his casual disregard of them. Any heightened regard for Zaria would cause trouble that could easily be avoided. Henrik really did need a wingman at times.

He stuffed the toast in his mouth and reached out for a plate of cold cuts. "Man, this looks great."

"Help yourself," Henrik said, bemused.

Wenche cleared her throat, reclaiming her son's attention. "This news you brought to us last night from Álfheim is most troubling. I don't understand what Queen Silje is thinking, leaving the goblins untouched. The forest is darker these days with shifting forces."

He nodded. "Olaf, the river-troll, has noticed similar activity along his waterways. The distance between Elleken and the Gjallarbrú is not far. You will need to watch your perimeter. Set an extra guard. Something isn't quite right, and until I get to the bottom of things, I want all of you to be on alert."

"Wouldn't it be best, if you stayed here?" she asked, resting a hand on his arm.

"I should be out there searching for answers," he evaded nimbly, as if this was a conversation they'd had before, more than once.

"What about protecting us?" she pressed.

"That's what I'd be doing," he stated firmly. "I'm much more useful out there than here."

146

She frowned and dropped her hand, busying herself preparing a small dish. "The fact that you think so is troubling to me and to your father. You're needed here. It's time you come home."

Zaria and Christoffer exchanged looks, but kept quiet, as Wenche handed Henrik the dish, which he accepted with a shrewd look directed at his mother. Studying her, he said, "It's not father at all. It's you who's worried; and I am home."

"He is your king," she reminded him. "He left you to see to duties he could not. You'll be staying, then?"

"Yes, he did, and I am," Henrik replied. "Mother, drop it. You have my answer. I am leaving you in charge in my absence."

"Be careful," she said, subsiding, resigned. "You are more precious to me than anything."

He pressed a kiss to her temple and hugged her close. "I will," he breathed against her hair, before straightening and standing. "Please prepare us food for the journey. I will come back as soon as I can."

"Of course. You know how to find us."

"You'll be moving?" he asked, head tipped to the side, taking in this new information.

She nodded. "I think that's best, don't you, with your absence? As you said, we're too close to the last sighting of these goblins."

"The move might be a little extreme," he cautioned. "Wouldn't you rather wait and get Silje's report?"

Wenche grimaced. "No, while a few sightings are normal and to be expected, their increased activity and ferocity requires vigilance. Even Olaf is concerned, you say, and you know what I think of him. So, I think, when you leave, we'll begin packing to go as well."

Henrik nodded in assent and walked out of the tent. Christoffer and Zaria followed, where they joined the others. Filip, saddened to miss breakfast, brightened considerably when he saw that Zaria had secured him something to eat in a cloth. Snacking and packing simultaneously, he rambled cheerfully while Henrik and Geirr left to try getting in touch with Bjarke or Olaf by the Gjallarhorn, Geirr with Aleks' horn.

Meanwhile, Aleks finished securing a missive to Airi's leg and sent her off with one last pet against the soft feathers of her head. She croaked and nipped at his fingers, taking flight. Her figure rose easily and disappeared from view. Like Aleks, Christoffer was going to miss her. She brought her own level of comedy to the group.

Two young ellefolken girls bounded over with Defender in tow, cuddling and kissing him. He soaked it all up and licked their faces causing them to squeal in laughter and hug him tighter. Henrik shooed them away with a few gentle words and a piece of salted black licorice.

The party gathered and readied, Henrik and Geirr having found some success in reaching the traveling river-trolls. Aleks took point and led them from Elleken with confidence and haste. Many came out to say goodbye, touching Henrik's sleeves and cloak, pressing parting gifts into his hands – sweets, flowers, nuts, berries, carvings, and even a pair of shoes and a soft lawn shirt with embroidered cuffs. Christoffer realized they must have been courting gifts, not unlike the ones from the night before to welcome him home. Henrik thanked each of them, until he could accept no more and gave his regrets.

As they disappeared into the trees, the ellefolken fell behind, turning to answer Wenche's orders to take down the tents. Henrik opened his bag, which started half empty, and deposited the tokens. His fingers gentled over the green ribbon tying up a small, soft cloth package, before he snapped the bag closed and slung it over his shoulder. Observing, Christoffer wondered if the green ribbon belonged to someone that had caught his friend's eye, or if he was simply touched by his people's generosity of spirit.

The trek northwest led them out of Gloomwood Forest and away from Elleken and Álfheim. All around them the forest breathed like a living entity, teeming to bursting with life and chatter from birds. The hiking path led them up and down and up again. As noon approached, they climbed a peak and saw the ocean in the nearby distance across a field of browning vegetation and stone.

The air was briny and crisp. A refreshing breeze lifted the wilted strands of Christoffer's hair. He breathed it in happily. Aleks shouted excitedly at seeing a large sailing ship with puffed sails on the distant horizon. It might be *Ursula* the very ship they were searching out. Their hike was nearly at the end. Olaf said Bjarke would wait for them offshore.

He and Zaria started to move down the slope when Henrik tugged them into slivers of shadows and motioned for everyone to be silent. Ahead of them a group of humans were busily gathering rotting vegetation and shrieking raucously amongst themselves. They appeared to be readying to leave.

Perplexed by Henrik's evasiveness, Christoffer moved to speak when the Stag Lord backed them further into the trees. The humans weren't going to care if they trekked past them to the ocean. He motioned to them, and whisper-said, "There's nothing to worry about, Henrik. Let's go."

"Look again," cautioned Henrik, nodding at the boisterous group.

There were about ten or so individuals, a mix of male and female, although the women outnumbered the men. Each one possessed a stunningly statuesque figure and sharply defined cheekbones, and dressed in simple homespun clothes. Their clothes were the only thing that struck Christoffer as odd, being severely out of fashion, and he kept trying to spot what had alarmed the Stag Lord.

He noticed next how fair was their skin, fairer than his, though they must've been outside for hours, and fairer still than Queen Silje's, whose pale hair was the color of corn silk. He could not make out their eye color from this distance, but it seemed dark. He did not mistake them for being related despite their similarities, though it was possible some were, indeed, kin.

"I don't get it," he said, shrugging. "What am I supposed to see?"

"Me either," admitted Zaria, which relieved Christoffer immensely. At least he wasn't the only one. A sidelong glance at the others showed equally baffled expressions.

"Keep watching," said Henrik, his dark tone alerting Defender.

The border collie gazed in the same direction, a low snarl building in his throat. His hackles rose, and he barked. Henrik clamped a hand on the dog, shushing him. Christoffer reached down to settle him, only to stop and stare, mouth agape.

The males below took great delight in shoving the unsuspecting females into the muck. One such unlucky female yanked an even unluckier male down beside her and pounced. She didn't do it with hand or foot. No, she used another limb. She did it with a tail that had previously been hidden under her skirt. A tail like that could only mean –

"Hulders?" he murmured, which Henrik confirmed, moving the group slowly away.

"Come," he said. "We need to go around."

"We'll miss the ship," protested Filip.

"We won't," assured Geirr. "They promised to wait."

"What are they doing?" whispered Zaria, lingering to watch.

Henrik also spoke in low undertones. "Courting, I think, but don't let them catch sight of you."

Filip stared at the frolicking group. "How come?"

"Hulders aim to seduce," Henrik said after clearing his throat. The noise traveled unexpectedly and the hulders glanced around curiously. Aleks pulled him back, as the others ducked. They held their breath. When the hulders returned to their game, he continued softly, "They sing to ensnare your senses and lure you to them. Then depending on their passions they may drink your blood or –"

"Do other stuff," supplied Aleks, dryly, crouching down and riffling in his bag.

Christoffer raised his eyebrows, but Zaria elbowed him, warning, "Don't start."

"I didn't say anything," he protested.

"Anything else to be aware of?" asked Geirr, peeking around the tree. "Venom? Inhuman strength? Super senses? Speed and endurance like an airplane?"

The Stag Lord balked, looking at him like he had two heads. "What are you going on about? No. They just delight in cruelty and mean-spirited pranks. When you're ensnared by their charms, they can make you think you're drinking milk when you're drinking urine, or you'll find that the delicious slice of pie you're eating is really animal feces with maggots."

"Speaking from experience?" Christoffer asked, snickering at the foul glare he received and a tightening around the eyes that to him loudly cried, "Yes, and don't ask me anything else."

"Here, everyone take a set," Aleks interrupted, opening his palm and revealing a fresh bag of earplugs.

"You came prepared," Zaria said, startled.

"I bet you feel useless," Christoffer said, and she skewered him with a glare. He was racking them up today. How many did that make now for his collection? Four? Five?

"Keep talking, mate," Filip said, smirking. "Dig the hole a little deeper."

"It's just a joke," he said, laughing it off. "I didn't mean anything by it. Zaria knows that."

"Shh," warned Henrik as the hulders stilled once more and looked about them.

The statuesque beings began to spread out and search the area. Struck by premonition, Christoffer hastily shoved the soft foam earplugs into his ears, and not a moment too soon, as their mouths opened and a muffled tune rang out. Filip and Geirr hadn't been quick enough with their earplugs and their eyes became unfocused, heads angling toward music Christoffer could only just make out.

*Come out, come out, littlest, tastiest, friend,*

*Intend ye to hide forever, be ye struck dumb?*

*Succumb to us, come and talk with us,*

*Fuss not, and we'll play the greatest game of pretend,*

*Wend ye now to us and it'll be fi, fi, fo, yum and then some.*

It was both enticing and creepy, like a glossy black spider singing to a succulent fly, and that was through the earplugs. Seeing his hapless friends begin to move forward, as if called by the music, Christoffer leapt forward to block their path.

With help from Henrik and Aleks wrangling them too, they were able to push them further back into the trees. All the while Filip and Geirr grappled with them sluggishly, eyes gazing longingly behind them, searching for the source of the siren song.

Zaria conjured over-the-ear headsets and slapped them over their heads. As they magically settled into place, their eyes lost that dazed look. Their bodies shook as a tremor passed through them simultaneously. Geirr stuffed his hands into his pockets and glared furiously at his shoes, as if they had offended him greatly.

Filip licked his lips, his expression still a little stunned, but more in fear than in enchantment. He gripped the headset and soft-shouted, "Noise canceling?"

Nodding, Zaria pressed a finger to her lips and gestured to Aleks. "Lead and we'll follow," she said.

He led, and they worked on completing their first evasion quest. The hulders scoured the grounds, slipping into the trees and over the exposed ground. They were neither faster, nor stronger, than Christoffer and the others, but they were as graceful and lithe as large cats and persistent in singing their compelling song, which grew more lyrics as it went, its tendrils creeping in lazy swirls to snag their senses.

Every so often the words slipped through and Christoffer or another would stumble. It was up to Filip and Geirr to rescue them when it happened, for Zaria – at the front with Aleks and an anxious Defender – was focused on the task of picking her way forward, leading the border collie by the collar, and didn't notice.

Christoffer finally knew what the witch of the woods had meant all those years ago about feeling the hulder's breath upon her. They hunted not with scent or sound or sight, but with a sense as integral to them as jokes were to him, except it wasn't funny. Not in the slightest. The hulders were unerringly good at guessing where their quarry scampered, and he had to dodge them often and backtrack to keep safely out of reach of their grasping lyrics.

Cursing, as a female appeared in front of him, his gaze darted around for escape. He couldn't think straight, and her magnetic beauty pulled his focus. She had long flowy golden hair with flowers upon her brow. Beckoning with a soft pink finger, she licked her ruby red lips, looking like she'd devoured a bushel of strawberries. They matched her glowing red eyes.

He tripped in his inattention and stumbled. Ducking and rolling, he worked to regain his footing. Standing, he noticed he'd lost an earplug in the process. Hurriedly he clapped his hands over his ears, but it was too late. Her honey-sweet voice slipped past his guard, and he was lost.

*Slow down, slow down, there's no need to shout and flee,*

*Be ye not alarmed. I am harmless, and not your foe.*

*Although, if you run, I guarantee,*

*Somebody will die, and it won't be I, my young beau.*

*Know ye are mine forever, and grant an eternal kiss to me.*

Inside he felt like screaming, but the terror, blocked by her singing, dampened. Then it melted away. He thought he should be scared. He had no control over his limbs, but he didn't think he should fight her too hard. She needed him. He lowered his hands. Her yearning notes became sharp and jagged as crystalline shards of glass. He wanted to soothe them. He knew how, too. His blood would be a salve to her and he was glad.

One step at a time, he found himself backing away from freedom, one simple shoreline away, and stepped toward her hungry, glittering gaze. She crooned to him, using her arms to gather him to her breast. His last glimpse of the sea, showed Geirr helping Henrik and Aleks into a waiting dinghy. He wanted to locate Zaria and Defender, but couldn't summon the strength to do it.

When Henrik spotted Christoffer's predicament, his eyes widened. He shouted something, but Christoffer heard only his captor's lilting voice, as she tipped up his chin and sighed a dewy breath against his parted lips. His arms curled around her, weaving into her hair, and he crept on tiptoe to reach her berry-red mouth.

An unknown force slammed into them, tumbling them to the ground. The music stopped, and the struggle began in earnest as fangs glistened wetly and lunged for his throat, snapping. He struggled to hold onto her, keen to accept the kiss she'd offered, while their unknown assailant hindered his every attempt. Seeing it was Filip, Christoffer and the girl snarled wordlessly at him, totally in sync.

"Look at her tail," Filip shouted, smacking Christoffer's hands away.

He pointed and Christoffer looked to where it bobbed irritably from under her skirt. The enchantment broke, and he gasped as sounds flooded his ears. He could hear the others by the boat shouting at him. He could hear Zaria struggling with other hulders, Defender barking and growling like mad beside her, as magic exploded all around, keeping the hulders from singing. Instead they snarled, red eyes flashing.

Helping Filip, he wrestled the hulder to the ground, kneeing her in the back. She struggled in vain, tossing her head this way and that. Catching his eye, she opened her mouth to appeal to him.

"Oh no you don't," he snapped at her, clapping a hand over her mouth.

"Run, mate, get to the water," Filip said. "She can't ensnare you again. You've seen her tail. Go!"

Christoffer didn't need telling twice. He took off, but he also dragged Filip up with him. Together they ran toward Zaria, and she flashed them a relieved grin as they slammed into her attackers, throwing them to the ground. Clutching at her hands, they propelled her forward. Defender fell in line, keeping close to his human and pack. They slipped over the sandy beach and plunged into the frigid waves. Hands hauled them up and over the side of the dinghy, and Christoffer collapsed, utterly spent.

"You okay, mate?" Filip asked, shaking him so hard his eyes opened. "She didn't kiss you, did she?"

"It was close, but no," he said, flinging an arm over his eyes, and in the darkness her red lips mocked him, beckoning him to claim a kiss. Abruptly he sat up and hugged his knees. "Thanks, man. We should do this again – make it more difficult, you know, like a no-damage run. I bet I could beat you this time."

Filip laughed, shaking his head. "While that sounds like fun, how about the next time you want a girlfriend, you don't go for one of those femme fatale types. She'll suck you dry, if you know what I mean. You'd be better off with one of those docile, doe-like ellefolken girls back at Elleken."

He groaned, flopping back again. "You're hilarious."

"I know," he said smugly. "Enough girl talk."

"But then what will you and Zaria have to say to each other?" he quipped.

Filip rolled his eyes and grinned. "Ready to rendezvous with some trolls, mate?"

# Chapter Eight: Elevated Tempers

The massive ship could easily ferry giants around Norway... well, young ones. An adult giant was probably nigh on impossible. *Ursula* sailed with rows and rows of brightly flapping white sails on soaring masts. She did not belabor her journey, but clipped along at a speedy pace, her red hull most likely aided by the river-troll who helmed her.

The crew consisted of ellefolken (females only for the obvious reasons) and elves (males and females), sporting eclectic almost steampunk-like outfits with brown leather skirts and aprons and billowy white shirts. They bustled about their duties in constant ebb and flow, much like the ocean lapping at the ship.

While the others explored *Ursula* and enjoyed the relative relaxation after their escape from the hulders, Christoffer meandered below deck to the galley. His thoughts circled round and round, back to the hulder he'd almost kissed, and he found it hard to snap back to the present. It was like her song still ensnared his senses.

In his mind's eye he lingered over her sultry red eyes and languid movements. She knew she had spellbound him. There had been no question, despite the middle of her stanza where she'd mentioned him trying to run. He recognized now the self-indulgent appetites long indulged and little curbed. She could not be reasoned with, and such rapacity scared him.

He had almost kissed her. He should be repulsed, but he couldn't quite muster up the energy for it. He wondered what it may have been like to taste her lips, to drink of her bitter potion. It gnawed at him from the insides causing him to shiver. Why had he wanted to kiss her? Was it simply her song? Was it more? He didn't want to dwell on it for fear of the answer.

The hot moist air of the galley washed over him, briefly clearing his senses of the lingering fog the remembrance of her song brought to him. He drifted into the center of the bustling room, finding a perch on a low-slung stool. As soon as he sat, a male elf thrust a sack of potatoes and a peeler at him. Christoffer nodded, acknowledging the unspoken request, and got to work, skinning with quick efficiency born from long hours spent in his mother's kitchen.

Finding his rhythm and his mental momentum, he soon got to the end of the sack and received the grudging admiration from the elf. He helped next preparing the fish and after that, the salad, and by then the meal had been completed. He grabbed a platter and followed everyone upstairs. Halfway to the mess hall Defender sprinted toward him, panting and eager.

"Down, boy. Stay down," Christoffer warned, shifting his platter away, as the border collie snuffled frantically at his knees and feet, before locking eyes on the source. "Down. Oof! No, boy. Bad. Bad, get off."

Little surprise when Defender cared not a jot and Christoffer nearly lost his balance along with the food, but another elf whisked it from his hands. He shoved Defender off and collared him, before he could make himself a nuisance again.

"Oh no you don't," he said, scratching behind the ears and getting a happy lick in response. "You better behave, or you're going to be water-wyvern bait."

"Where have you been?" asked Zaria poking her head around the doorframe.

"Down in the galley." He stood, keeping a staying hand on top of his dog, adding cheekily, "Miss me?"

She grabbed his sleeve and tugged him down the hall toward the crowded mess. "Silly goose, of course we missed you, but I'm sure you needed that time and space apart to work out how you're feeling. You won't get that luxury off the boat, so I encouraged everyone to leave you alone. Did I do the right thing?"

Running a hand over his lightly gelled spikes, Christoffer said quietly, "That hulder and I nearly traded saliva. I – I wasn't grossed out."

Zaria looked at him, considering what he said and left unsaid. "It's all right, you know. Even I thought the males were attractive. They're meant to be – it's how they entice their prey. It wasn't until I spied a tail on one that I saw his true face."

Canting his head inquiringly, he asked, "True face? Hers didn't look any different to me after I saw her tail. Her voice however lost its compulsion."

She shrugged. "Henrik explained that the males are actually quite ugly. This one had a large, aquiline nose and sagging jowls."

"Like a reverse frog prince. Kiss, and surprise! He's uglier than ever."

"When I saw his true nature, he clutched his face in despair. I pitied him," she said, and he knew she understood his conflicting emotions. She had her own, too.

Christoffer finally got why he was haunted by his experience. He wanted to believe in her, the hulder who nearly had him, to think she was capable of good. For the hulders looked human, just like the elves, fairies, and ellefolken. But they didn't want to be good, and delighted in wickedness and mischief. He and Zaria would have to remember that when facing them again. Something told him the time would come sooner rather than later.

He had to break the somber mood. It was too heavy. Nudging her side, he said, "What does a vegetarian werewolf say to the moon?"

She blinked, coming back from her faraway thoughts, a smile beginning to bloom. "No idea. What does a vegetarian werewolf say to the moon?"

"Arrrru-gula!" he howled.

She laughed, and he grinned. When one could laugh the world was brighter. She took a seat at the far end of the table. He joined her, opposite Filip. The meal was served family style, and the room filled up. Elves, ellefolken, the trolls, and his friends sat around gossiping and swapping stories.

"Aye, we'll be in Jötunheim by midafternoon tomorrow," said Bjarke, *Ursula's* portly and affable captain, who, like Olaf, had all the hallmarks of a river-troll sans the river – dark reflective eyes, muddled blue and brown scales, claw-tipped webbed fingers, and pointy, drooping nose.

"Be you reconsidering my request?" asked Olaf, as the crew dwindled in the mess, leaving the trolls and Christoffer and his friends behind.

Bjarke eyed him warily, rubbing a hand over his rotund form. "Nay."

"You fool," swore Olaf. "It be just like two hundred years ago. Did not the ellefolken and elves be helping you when he came for you? Cousin, help me now."

Bjarke's river once ran tributary to Olaf's; in their world, that made them cousins. Christoffer wasn't certain how Bjarke survived without a river, but he thought it had to do with *Ursula* herself, and not dissimilar to how Olaf survived on a new river after altruistically surrendering the Gjöll for the schemes to imprison the dragons in the Under Realm.

Bjarke's small fangs disappeared with a grimace. "I am helping ye. Am I not taking ye to Oskar the

Elevated? It's all I can promise ye. Nay, don't ask of me anything more."

"My river be shrinking," pressed Olaf, tapping the table with a sharp claw. "Christoffer be able to tell you. He be seeing it for himself."

"Your river is shrinking?" Zaria asked, looking between him and the trolls. "What does that mean?"

"We think it means a dragon attack," said Christoffer, before leaning out across the table to look at the captain. "Olaf's melting the hidden frozen places in his river to keep the levels high."

"You be knowing what comes next," warned Olaf.

Bjarke closed his eyes and shuddered. "Yer waters will corrupt. They will gray."

Henrik's eyes widened with understanding. He met Olaf's penetrating gaze. "The trees will grow twisted and dark," he breathed.

Olaf dipped his chin. "You not be with heir. You not be able to save me like your grandfather did for him."

Two hundred odd years ago, Henrik's grandfather saved Bjarke, whose river had been infected by the dragon Ægil. Not much more was known about what happened – for Bjarke, traumatized, preferred not to speak of it, and Hakon, now a tree, couldn't speak of it in a more literal sense.

Henrik had no children, and thus couldn't join the ranks of the Golden Kings to rescue a decaying forest. He could not prop up the barrier between the Under Realm and the world. There would be no recourse from that quarter. Fate had caught up with the ellefolken. Their Stag Lord could not perform the duties expected of him. What that might mean for Olaf and Norway, Christoffer couldn't begin to guess.

"There has to be something else Henrik can do," Christoffer said; after all, his friend was the hero, and heroes were never without options.

"Surely, turning into a tree isn't the only answer," added Geirr when nobody spoke.

Zaria bit her lip, thinking. "There must be something we can do to reverse the changes. Perhaps my mother or I —"

Olaf rested his hand over Zaria's. "Everything be working out in the end. Hold onto faith. Besides, it not be a sorceress' magic that I be needing."

"You need another river-troll's," guessed Christoffer.

"I'll not be doing it," said Bjarke. "I got out of the business of rivers, and I'm not going back."

"Cousin," growled Olaf. "If you not be willing to come to my headwaters, then gift to me the magic."

"I will not diminish my powers," Bjarke insisted, shoving back from the table. "There be more dangers in the open sea than on a river, even a river with a dragon's attentions."

"What's worse than a dragon?" asked Filip.

Geirr frowned at the captain. "I thought dragons were the most dangerous beings on earth. Evil."

"My cousin be a superstitious fool," sneered Olaf, also shoving back his seat. He pressed his nose into Bjarke's face. "The last time a kraken be seen in these waters be back when Leif Eriksson sailed to the new world. He be a fearful old goat."

"Bahhhh," Bjarke mocked.

"Please, let's be civil," begged Zaria. "Olaf, you must realize what a hard ask you put before Bjarke."

"Even yer little princess agrees."

She stared at him. "Bjarke, you must know that Olaf wouldn't ask if the situation wasn't dire."

"Ha! She be agreeing with me," retorted Olaf with a smirk.

"It will never happen," Bjarke declared and swept from the room, effectively shutting the conversation down.

"That sure didn't go well," Christoffer said.

"Instead of saying nothing and getting nowhere, these two boneheads said too much and got worse than nowhere," said Geirr.

"We should all go get some fresh air," said Henrik, motioning to Olaf to go before him.

The next morning found Christoffer on top of a mizzenmast with Filip and Aleks as the boat plunged through rough waters. Airi had left ages ago, at the first sign the weather would turn foul. She sped daily messages to Aleks, aided by their close proximity to Niffleheim.

Poor Geirr huddled next to the rail midship, struggling to keep from puking his guts on deck. Zaria kept him company and even conjured a bucket for him at one point. Henrik stood next to the helmsman, who deftly angled the ship toward the harbor of Seiland Island.

Christoffer eyed the water excitedly, expecting to spot a pod of humpback whales he had seen before. Wherever he looked, though, nothing appeared below the water's surface but the shadow of the ship itself. He sulked, wondering where they'd gone.

"Do you see them? Where are they?" he asked.

Aleks shook his head. "I don't see anything."

"Over there," shouted Filip, pointing. "They're blocking the harbor."

"Why would they be doing that?" asked Aleks, frowning, and peering at the whale blockade preventing them from going closer.

The ship dipped and rolled heavily in the water filling the channel. Wind billowed the sails and pushed the ship closer and closer. The island's soaring cliff faces dwarfed the massive ship. As they watched from their perch, a piece of rock sheared off, plummeting into the sea, sending out a gigantic rolling wave.

"Hang on tight," warned Aleks, as it approached with unbroken speed.

At impact, the ship lurched sideways, forcing Christoffer to cling to the mast for dear life. "Why would a cliff just collapse like that?"

"It's not a cliff," said Filip. "It's a giant."

"You're joking," said Aleks.

"I'm the comedian around here," said Christoffer, watching the rock unfurl itself and stand up.

"You're not joking," breathed Aleks.

At his full height, the water lapped around the giant's waist. His arms were crossed, and he glowered down at the ship. His thunderous face was full of pits and crags, the deep blue-gray of the rock glistening wetly from the recent dip. The whales circled him and the harbor's opening, keeping their distance.

"Why is he scowling at us? What did we do?" asked Filip, pushing back his hair and bracing against the wind's fury.

The sky overhead lowered with pent-up menace as thunderclouds hung heavy, full of rain. Lightning streaked across the sky, followed closely by foreboding cracks of thunder. The ship swung to starboard, presenting its flanks to the giant as Bjarke bellowed orders to the crew. Christoffer and his friends were shooed off the mast. Anchors were loosed, sails came down, and ropes were lashed and tied all around the deck.

Huddling on deck next to Geirr and Zaria, Christoffer peered under the sky's onslaught, fighting not to shiver from the cold wind and sideways rain. The giant hadn't moved an inch, nor had he spoken. Bjarke lowered a tender into the water and settled in with Olaf and Henrik. It scuttled through the waves, disappearing and reappearing with every dip and roll.

"You're not welcome, be gone," intoned the giant in deep, rumbling speech.

"Is that Ingdor?" questioned Zaria, poking her head out from under her conjured umbrella. She fought to keep it steady against the onslaught of wind, determined to rip it out of her hands. It inverted and jerked from her grasp, pitching over the rail and falling into the water below.

"I think so, though his face is pitted with scars now. Come here," said Filip, tucking Zaria into his side and surrounding her with his jacket.

"Thanks," she murmured, pressing her face into his warmth and tucking her hands under his shirt.

"Jeez, Zar-Zar, your hands are like ice," he said, shivering.

Across the way, Ingdor's voice boomed, shaking the tender carrying Olaf, Henrik, and Bjarke. "Oskar closed the island to outsiders."

"That's bad timing. Why do you think he shut down the island?" asked Aleks, standing straight and tall, his sea legs keeping him balanced.

"It's not a coincidence," Christoffer said, bracing against the railing as the ship rolled once more, dipping and tilting precariously.

"Zaria can't you control the weather?" Geirr moaned, leaning weakly against the railing.

"I don't know that I've ever tried before," she said amused.

"Why not?" asked Christoffer. "I would. You're only limited by your imagin—"

"Christoffer," warned Aleks, cutting him off.

Nodding to acknowledge his slip of tongue, he continued, "You could create lightning or hail storms or hurricanes, I'm certain of it."

"I'm really only good at conjuring and banishing things," Zaria said. "Also, that seems dangerous."

Christoffer sent her a disbelieving look. "How would you know? You just admitted to not even trying."

"I don't mean dangerous to myself. I just mean, I don't have anything against rain. What if stopping it means it wouldn't start again unless I made it start? What then? Am I responsible for the whole world's weather patterns? I'm not cut out to be the world's weather woman."

"You can't really believe that, can you? Magic isn't limiting, it's limitless."

"Just because something is doable, doesn't mean you *should* do it."

"How about, then, because it's fun?"

"When would she practice doing that?" countered Aleks, who'd been listening and nodding along to everything Zaria said. "At school, while we're going between classes? Or how about at home under her parents' supervision?"

"There's a time. There's a place," he argued, thinking not for the first time that the two shared such a fundamental belief in how magic should be used. It was so unfair they were the ones who could do it.

"Not that much time," said Filip, winking at Zaria.

"Ugh, gross," Christoffer joked, graciously giving up on the idea of elemental magic... for now.

"You're both impossible," Zaria teased, rolling her eyes, but smiling.

Their conversation got interrupted by another booming declaration from Ingdor. "Oskar the Elevated is unavailable for consultation."

Olaf's words carried over the wind as it buffeted. "I be bearing important news that cannot wait. Olaf carry Queen Helena's token. Do you see?"

The giant bent, drawing closer, only to stop without ever looking when a giantess shouted from the top of the cliffs. "Brother, they are banned from setting foot on the island."

"Banned?" everyone seemed to echo at once.

That was different from the island being closed presumably due to bad weather. Why would Oskar banish them from his kingdom? Wouldn't he want their trade? Isn't that what made Seiland Island, in part, the High Court of Jötunheim? Was something going on that he didn't want them to find out? Or had they somehow offended him?

"The trade," said Geirr, looking at them with baleful eyes, before closing them and swallowing nervously as the ship floor surged beneath him.

Aleks rubbed his back soothingly. "Deep breaths, nice and easy. You're okay. You can do this."

"What trade?" asked Zaria.

Geirr gestured weakly, but didn't speak.

"Oskar didn't accept our trade before and we left without permission," Filip recalled, pushing his hair away from his face.

Shielding his eyes from the rain, Christoffer glanced toward the giantess on the cliff. "He's what – angry with us? Why does everyone seem to hold grudges against us? Where's the logic in that? We saved the realms twice from dragons."

A pensive look crossed Zaria's face. "We need to offer a trade he can't refuse."

"One small problem with that plan. How will we make amends if he doesn't grant us an audience?" asked Geirr.

"He has to see Olaf. After all, the troll wasn't part of our entourage last time," Christoffer pointed out, gripping the rail in a hurry as the ship dipped.

"Do we care?" asked Aleks, shifting to redistribute his weight. "We're not here for him, but for the raven which is somewhere nearby."

"I only care to get off this blasted boat," Geirr groaned, his head sagging. "Use a coin and wish us out of here."

"No way," Christoffer shot down. "You've never done it, but trust me when I say fire-travel is wicked hot. Like hotter than your favorite sauna in the dead of winter with the door welded shut. Like so hot you wish you could bathe in lava to cool off, hot. Besides you see this hair? It takes real effort to get it this nice. I'd like it to stay unsinged, thank you very much. That, and burnt hair smell are the worst."

"Can you teleport?" asked Aleks, looking at Zaria who gazed at Geirr with concern.

"I can try," she said meekly, now looking a little worried for herself.

Filip offered her a steadying hand for support as she fixed her sights on the rocky cliffs behind Ingdor and his whales. The air pulled tight and taut. Static energy built along the hairs on Christoffer's arms and with a brief shock disappeared, along with Zaria. A grin spread across his face as he looked at his friends and then turned his attention to the cliffs. The air darkened at one spot and with a crackle of purple energy Zaria appeared.

"Wooooo!" cheered Christoffer, throwing his hands in the air.

He grabbed Geirr by the elbows and danced a merry jig, much to the other's consternation and resistance. A moment later that sizzle of static erupted along his skin to burst away when Zaria made her reappearance. He hoisted her up in a bear hug that had her laughing and hitting his shoulders in a soft protest.

"Put me down, Christoffer!" she squealed.

"Zaria, you're amazing. Has anyone told you how amazing you are lately? Because you are amazing, like super amazing!"

She was laughing as he set her down. Filip slung an arm along her shoulders and grinned, bending down to buss her open mouth. "You are amazing, Zar-Zar," he told her, chucking her lightly beneath the chin and causing her to blush. She hid her face briefly against his neck before pulling back.

"Let's hurry," said Aleks. "Ingdor's distracted."

Zaria took them over one by one, starting with Geirr. Once on the cliffs, he sat abruptly, remaking his acquaintance with the ground. Christoffer went second, and the sensation of teleporting squeezed all the air out of his lungs, not dissimilar to how Olaf's transportation felt inside his realm between bubbles. He wondered if Zaria copied it, basing her style on the troll's. Before he could come to a conclusion, the journey ended, quick and painless, despite the discomfiting sensation of losing all the air in his lungs.

When Aleks, Filip, and Zaria arrived, they stumbled on the landing, losing their footing and crashing into each other. Despite the rain, Filip, who looked like he'd stuck a finger in a socket, got to his feet first and offered each a hand, hoisting them upright in a trice. Zaria battled the wind for control of her hair, as a looming shadow fell across them.

Christoffer glanced up into a truly frightening visage. He gulped. "Uh, hi?"

"Princess, you were warned," came an ugly, angry voice, slow and threatening. "You and your friends are not welcome in my kingdom."

# Chapter Nine: The White Raven's Mourning

"Why is that?" Zaria asked, conjuring a fresh umbrella and hoisting it high above her head. "I should think that the High King of Jötunheim would welcome a contingent with representation from Niffleheim, Elleken, and the Under Realm."

The foreboding giant simmered like an active volcano, heat waves practically radiating above his rocky skin. He took his time to formulate his reply, a defining hallmark of his people. When he spoke, the finality of his words held more weight because of his deliberation.

"Niffleheim's return to Norway is fledging at best and insincere at worst. The fey, not the giants, must prove themselves. Respect is earned, not granted upon lip service.

"The previous Stag Lord, voice of the ellefolken, slipped away in the dead of night like a criminal. Raised as a prince and now an adult, he knew our traditions and culture, but chose to ignore both to selfishly serve his own needs.

"Then there's you, Princess," he intoned darkly, causing Zaria to flinch. "The last time you were in my kingdom you dealt me a grave insult. I waited for a formal apology that never came. There is bad blood between us, and only when I receive satisfaction can the damage begin to be reversed."

Tilting her head back, Zaria canvassed the scene before her. Christoffer wondered if the looming presence of six glowering giants intimidated her. It intimidated him. Not one did he recognize, and each craggy, inhuman face reared darker and more forbidding than the last, culminating with Oskar the Elevated, king of the giants, whose anger poured from him like a living thing.

He, by far, was the most terrifying of the bunch. His scowl was so deeply etched into his forehead it made his eyes shadowy black holes, sucking away all light and warmth. Christoffer hadn't thought to be frightened of the giants before despite their size, but now it was all he could do not to hide like some small frightened animal. Zaria must be quivering in her tennis shoes. This was not the Jötunheim they knew.

The last time they'd been to Seiland, the giants had been among the friendliest beings in magical Norway, slow of speech and big of heart, even if Oskar and Seila had been inclined to deny them aid in reaching the dwarf kingdom of Jerndor. The giant rulers had not wanted the Drakeland Sword to be in play again fearing it might wind up in the wrong hands and lead to disaster. Oskar was wrong then, but if he were to know the fate of the sword now... talk about a disaster.

Zaria stood her ground facing her accuser. "There was bad blood on all sides back then."

Oskar's eyes narrowed. "I beg your pardon."

"As a host, you were not the most welcoming," she elaborated.

Oskar snatched her up, peering angrily at her bedraggled figure, her umbrella nearly poking out his baseball-size eye. He growled, "Not welcoming? How dare you utter such a falsehood! You left without so much as a by your leave, forwent the customary trade, and convinced two of my young giants to be insubordinate."

"Now hold on one minute," Filip said, striding forward. "Trade was offered, which you declined."

Aleks nodded and crossed his arms. "I recall your deafness to all pleas to provide support, essentially telling a father his son deserved to die for the sake of your safety."

"Because you deemed a sword too dangerous to be put back into service," Geirr threw in, matching the fey king's stance, forming a bookend set.

"A sword, mind you, which neither belonged to you, nor was in your possession for safekeeping," chided Christoffer, sweeping back his hair and blinking away rain. He met the stares of the giants surrounding them one by one. "All we needed was safe passage and for you to vouch for us to the king of Jerndor. Not exactly taxing endeavors."

Unwilling to be manhandled further, Zaria transported out of Oskar's brutal grasp, returning to stand beside Christoffer. Her purple eyes flashed. "You essentially made us prisoners, just because we didn't abide by your agenda. You refused the trade to keep us from saving an innocent from a terrible plot.

Had you succeeded, he would be dead, Hector could not have transformed into a Golden King, and the Under Realm would have fallen to Koll."

The giants surrounding Oskar rumbled in confusion even as his countenance darkened. "You say many words, children, and all of them false."

"We could really use your sister right about now," Christoffer mumbled under his breath to Aleks. "She'd call him out on his cra —"

"Prove it," Zaria said, holding out her hands palms upturned, as if to catch something. "I have brought you something in trade to observe the social niceties. Will you accept it in return for an answer to a single question? Afterward we will leave and stay away until invited back to Seiland."

Oskar contemplated her small form, suspicion ripe on his face. Slowly, and after much deliberation, he dipped his head in assent. At his acceptance, an object appeared in her hands. It was a small metal flute, which she set on the ground, enlarging it with a wave of her hand to fit comfortably in the giant's grip. He picked it up and examined it, giving it a cursory blow. It sounded like a foghorn to Christoffer, and he covered his ears.

"The proportions are right," she told the giant ruler. "For it to sound as good as human-sized flutes you will just need to practice."

Oskar passed the flute to one of the nearby giants. "What is your question?" he asked.

She smiled. "Where can we find the talking white raven that belonged to one of your giants?"

"With the Lonely One. Now go. Astral, escort them to your brother. He will take you back to your ship."

"That's it?" demanded Geirr. "That's hardly an answer at all."

"That is hardly a musical instrument," Oskar replied, indicating Zaria's gift. "A fair enough trade, don't you think?"

"Come," a figure from the back said woodenly. The giantess emerged from behind the others, eyes downcast, and a frown permanently creased across her brow. She looked miserable and withdrawn, not at all the booming, confident giantess she'd been at their last meeting. Oskar had not forgiven her, or her brother, it seemed.

"Astral," Filip called, jogging over to greet her. "It's been a while. How are you?"

She frowned harder. "Fine."

"No fraternizing," warned Oskar and she cut him a quick glance, inclining her head minutely.

"Of course, your Elevated," she said, and turned away, starting down the mountain cliff.

Everyone else was left to fend for themselves, stumbling along a treacherous and steep path down to the harbor. Christoffer slipped more than once on loose stones and had to scramble for purchase. He even grabbed Geirr's collar when the teen almost fell off the cliff, nearly choking him.

"Thanks," he sputtered, righting himself.

When they were safely out of sight, Zaria began speaking rapidly. "I don't understand what is going on here at all. Astral, what has happened to the giants? It feels like Trolgar did under Jorkden."

"The Seiland giants have lost their queen."

"Oh no, poor Oskar," cried Zaria. "No wonder he's being so beastly. He is grieving."

"How did you lose her?" demanded Aleks. "Did she transform?"

Astral nodded. "She did. It began during the battle of Koll's Bane. Oskar tried to get her home in time, but he failed. Now she can never come home. She'll remain forever apart. Oskar blames –"

"Zaria," Christoffer supplied knowingly. "That's rotten, but it would have been worse had Koll won."

"If you hadn't taken up the sword, it wouldn't have happened at all," Astral said after a pause, stepping across a divide too wide for them to follow.

"Yes, it would have," said Geirr, accepting the giantess' help to cross. "It would have been worse."

"We will never know."

"Did you lose others?" Filip asked. "There seemed so many new faces. Where were Lohcca, Ello, and Rikkar? Surely Oskar would have listened to their council in the face of his wife's absence."

"Transformed," answered Astral. At their frozen looks she added. "Naturally."

"Are the others new to Seiland or recruits from other tribes?" asked Christoffer. "They seem angrier than the giants I am used to."

"Some of them are new to Seiland. When giants transform, it's not long before newborns walk among us. Most have taken up Oskar's rhetoric."

"But not you," said Aleks.

They neared the beach and she turned to address them. "There's a change in Jötunheim that I dread, but I am already on shaky ground for helping you during your last visit. You will find there are no friends here and no paths toward understanding."

"Guys, this is bad," said Filip, stating the obvious. "We have to warn Olaf about what he's up against. If Oskar won't heed him, because he's angry and blames us for Seila –"

"Do not mention her name," warned Astral, beckoning to her brother across the sea.

"Why not? Isn't that her name?" asked Filip.

Aleks shook his head. "I've just gone over this with Saskia and Nori. Once transformation is complete the name returns to the giants' book of names for the next giant to bear. They believe that if you use the name after transformation, you're hindering a new giant from forming."

"It's not belief," Astral said.

"But it's not like you name the next to be born giant after the one who just departed either, so how do you know?"

"We know because the calculations fail to resolve, and the previous giant experiences unrest unable to fully meld back into the mountains," she replied, hailing her brother.

Ingdor waded slowly toward them, the seas frothing and crashing all around him even as the whales created a gap for him to slide through. "Sister, how did these visitors come to you? I was in the harbor."

Astral waved a hand toward Zaria. "The sorceress."

He frowned. "Does Oskar blame me?"

She shrugged. "He wants you to escort them back to their ship. They are not to return."

"The queen sorceress' emissary is requesting a meeting with Oskar."

"The island is closed," she reminded him.

He sighed, beleaguered. "You try telling a river-troll he's unwelcome. See how far you get."

Dark shapes hovered over the cliff high above, watching them. Astral lowered her voice. "Go. You must go now."

"Wait," said Christoffer, even as Ingdor scooped him up with the others. "We need to know about the Lonely One. Where can we find him?"

Ingdor transferred them to his shoulders and began the slow return to the tender, still hovering in the middle of the harbor. "Hang on tight, especially you, Princess."

"Ingdor," Christoffer whined. "You can't ignore me. We're buds remember?"

A low, rumbling chuckle escaped the giant. He glanced upward at those watching from the cliffs and schooled his features into a thundering frown. "I'm sorry, young human. We are not friends, not now, but maybe again in the future. This shall pass. We must wait out his mourning and his temper."

"The Lonely One?" pressed Christoffer.

"Bjarke will know," he said, regret and sadness dripping from every word.

"I will know what?" shouted the river-troll, as he leaned out of the tender to grasp the first of the giant's burdens – Christoffer's friends.

"The Lonely One," said Zaria, hurriedly taking a seat in the bobbing tender. Henrik steadied her, and she smiled gratefully at him.

"Be Oskar granting Olaf's request?" demanded Olaf, working with Bjarke to bring everyone onboard.

"I'm afraid not," said Ingdor.

"It be unacceptable," fumed the troll, working the ring on his finger angrily.

"You're one of the ones he blames for losing his wife," said the giant, dropping Christoffer into the troll's waiting arms.

"Why don't I feel just like a damsel," teased Christoffer, earning a grimace from Olaf.

"Then I must be going and making my amends," said Olaf, depositing Christoffer none too gracefully. "Take me now, there be not another moment to lose. Dragons are afoot."

"Jötunheim cares not about dragons," informed the giant, but the troll heeded him not.

Olaf left with Ingdor despite everyone's protests, including the giant's. He had a task to do, and he was going to complete it. Bjarke promised to return for him in two days' time. Everyone else returned to *Ursula*, and the anchor was lifted. The troll captain knew where to drop them off to find the Lonely One, having often used the transformed giant as a landmark. It wasn't far which was a good thing, since Geirr was ready to leave the ship moments after setting foot on it.

Defender, too, was happier to be on the beach once they got there. He ran its length, kicking up sand and rolling in muddied puddles amongst the grasses. The ellefolken team who rowed them to shore promised to wait for their Stag Lord until the captain called for them to return for Olaf. Henrik grasped their palms in thanks. One girl nearly swooned, but another with a scar slashing through her eyebrow elbowed the fainter, earning a shriek of protest. She grinned wickedly and winked at Christoffer. He winked back.

Speaking softly as they departed, Henrik revealed intel gained with Ingdor and Bjarke while the two groups had been separated. "The Seiland giants call him the Lonely One, his old name being left unspoken, –"

"We learned that, too, with their queen," said Zaria, looking depressed. "The names are returned to the annals of their naming book."

"Yes, but unlike the queen, this fellow in particular evokes the giants' sadness, as his solitude is at odds with the giants' normal inclination for hearth and home. They can accept that their queen is lost to them due to war, because it was beyond choice. But he chose to transform away from them –"

"I don't blame him one bit," said Geirr. "Not with a petty giant ruling them. I thought intelligence was highly prized by the giants in their rulers. Oskar is showing none."

"Oskar managed to bring his queen to the foot of a mountain south of us. She is amongst her kind, if not her tribe. There is some solace there. Giants are not meant to be alone. The Lonely One separating from them is a tragic loss. They're not sure if his name will re-enter the book at all for another's use."

As the rain began to diminish and the clouds to disperse, a familiar white raven appeared on the breeze and cried out in greeting, "Eye-riii!" After a brief exchange, a nuzzle or two, and respite on Aleks shoulder, she took to the skies again with his directions in her ear. She flew ahead, leading the way, her shadow tracing faintly along the ground as they followed. Twilight fell and held as the sun danced low in the sky.

Christoffer and the others came upon the Lonely One on the mainland. They grew quiet, observing his reduced form where it sat next to a small, dark pond. The barren, browning landscape surrounding him stretched out into the distance, rolling and unchanging as far as the eye could see. The Lonely One epitomized isolation, and his friend, the white raven who had bonded with him in life, was his only company. Nothing stirred.

They were told the raven called at dusk for his old master. Straining, they heard nothing, until one long bleat broke through the stillness. The low, mournful cry tore at Christoffer, like a sadness without end. If sound had a color and shape, it would be as nacreous as a mollusk shell and as small as a pearl. It was the sound of tears dripping from eyes which could not or should not cry. So deeply scored was the loss... it occurred to Christoffer that it was the raven, and not the giant, who was lonely.

Airi who had been flying in lazy loops landed abruptly, clutching at Aleks' leather-clad shoulder. "Don't be sad," she called, and the cries stopped.

The silence changed. It now felt watchful and more than a bit wary. Christoffer searched for the raven, trying to spy him in his hiding spot. The transformed giant, now more hill than person in shape, had a few trees growing on his head, which twisted backwards, as if listening to someone call his name. The raven wasn't in their bare scraping limbs.

What once had been an ear was now a shallow cave, probably home to a small diurnal creature. Long, flat rocks dotted the hill like stepping stones, or perhaps vertebrae, offering an easy climb to the top. One inset rock looked like an open, vacant, unseeing eye – it gave Christoffer a start. Yet, the raven was not seen in any of these places.

Grass struggled up through the rocky surface where the top of his head would be. Bowers of fading flowers shimmered and swayed in the wind, forming facial hair. There in its shadows, under the chin, perched the white raven. Upon being spotted, it flew up into the shifting limbs and eyed them beadily, assessing the group.

"Who are you? Why are you here?" it chattered down to them in a honk-like fashion.

"Good evening, my feathered friend," said Henrik, tilting his face up to the bird. "I'm Henrik, Stag Lord of the ellefolken. My friends and I have journeyed far to find you."

"Princeling, why do you seek me out? Be it counsel, knowledge, or adjudication?"

"I have a friend who desperately desires a white raven, – one of your intelligence and standing."

"Tell your friend I'm not interested," it croaked, fluttering to a higher branch. "Go away, elk, and leave me in peace."

Geirr eyed the raven in speculation. Pitching his voice low, he asked, "Is it me, or is this white raven exceptionally loquacious?"

"It's not you," said Aleks, thinking hard, while stroking the top of his raven's feathered crown. "What I don't know is if his speech is normal. Will Airi sound like that? What do you think Stag Lord?"

"Hard to say," said Henrik. "I agree with Geirr, though, that this raven has a singular grasp on speech. It's like nothing I've ever heard or would expect."

During their speech, the raven canted its head, trying to listen to them above the wind. He hopped up and down in agitation. "Speak up," he demanded.

"Certainly," called Henrik, waving grandly and sweeping his cloak aside. "Let me introduce you to my companions. This is Princess Zaria of the Under Realm. Over there is King Aleks of Niffleheim with his white raven Airi. These gentlemen beside me are —"

"I'm Christoffer," he said, interrupting. He looked down and patted his furry friend. "And this is my dog, Defender. Next to Zaria is Filip and beside Aleks is Geirr. What's your name?"

"Vassals? Slaves? Subjects? Servants?"

Zaria laughed and shook her head, tucking a stray hair behind her ear. "Hardly. They're our friends."

"Friends with humans?" puzzled the raven. "How odd and rebellious of you, Princess. I'm Skorri."

"Sorry?" Christoffer asked, a mischievous glint twinkling in his eye.

"Skorri," the raven repeated irritably.

He cupped his ear. "Sorry, can you repeat that?"

"I said my name is Skorri."

"Eh? Sorry, I didn't catch that."

"Skorri, I'm Skorri."

"No need to be sorry, just tell us your name."

"Christoffer!" Zaria admonished, and he laughed dancing out of reach of her grasping hands. She shook her head and tipped it back to look the raven in the eye. "It's a pleasure to meet you."

"I can't say the same, but now that we've all been introduced, kindly go away and don't return. You're not welcome here."

"This is becoming a common refrain today," muttered Geirr.

"You're telling me," said Christoffer.

# Chapter Ten: Skorri's Challenge

A short while later the group's frustration level had risen to new heights: the giant's white raven stymied them at every conversational gambit and with every chatty overture. Extremely annoyed, Christoffer was saved from saying something he'd regret to the mouthy bird by Defender retuning with a stick, his tail wagging eagerly. Taking it, he hurled it as far away as he could, while Airi tried, yet again, to gain Skorri's attention and conversation. She failed.

"Your Airi is unimpressive," croaked Skorri, eyeing Aleks with contempt. "Her speech is primitive and coarse. No. No. I won't go."

"She picked up talking within days," protested Aleks. "She's smart, and loyal, and brave."

"She's your dog then, is she?" sneered Skorri. "Does she relieve herself on command?"

"He didn't mean that, Defender," Christoffer said, kneeling and giving his dog a good scratching. He got a low woof and a lick on his face.

Skorri harrumphed. "That was rhetorical. No. No. Leave me and never return."

Christoffer ignored him, lavishing praise on his canine friend. "You're the best doggie there is. He can't insult Airi or us, can he? No, he can't, because you are smart, and loyal, and brave."

"Airi is ten times the raven you are," Aleks muttered in a surly undertone, gaining her approving nip on his ear.

"Guys, should we be insulting him?" Geirr asked, watching the raven above with misgiving. "We want him to come with us."

"That one is smart," said Skorri, peering down from his perch with one beady eye. He raised his foot and scratched his neck. "You should listen to him."

"Stupid raven," squawked Airi, clicking her beak.

His feathers puffed out. "Bird brain. Just look at you, you witless drudge, you fowl dullard. Your voice is rough. It grates on my ears. If you don't go away, I will. I swear I will."

"Promises, promises," murmured Christoffer, winking at Airi. She hooted, clicking her beak in appreciation.

Aleks growled, unable to bear the insult. "Listen here, you ill-mannered cretin, –"

"You wouldn't though," said Henrik, staying the fey king. He tossed his backpack onto the ground and unfastened his cloak.

"Wouldn't what?" Skorri asked despite himself.

"Leave."

Filip settled his and Zaria's bags on the ground beside Henrik's, sighing with relief upon standing free of their strain. He shielded his eyes from the glare of the sun peeking through the branches. "You know, we could camp here forever and still you wouldn't leave."

"You must have loved your giant very much," Zaria said, joining Filip.

Geirr followed suit, chucking his bag against the others, and even went so far as to unroll his sleeping bag under the white raven's baleful scowl. "I bet you stick around so you can keep talking to him, don't you? Isn't it lonely? How can you be sure he hears you? He never answers back."

Skorri bobbed up and down in agitation. "He hardly ever spoke. He loved to listen. I gave him news, gossip, messages, stories, and music. I must keep him company. Who would talk to him, if I didn't?"

"Would he want you to stay? He would want you to find someone you could talk to, just as you did with him, because even if he hardly ever spoke, still, he did speak. One-sided conversations must be hard on you," Zaria said, kicking off her shoes and settling down. She patted the ground beside her for Filip, and he collapsed in an ungraceful heap, groaning in pleasure as his muscles relaxed.

"We'll be right back," Christoffer said and then whistled for Defender.

"I'll join you," said Aleks, and Airi trilled her agreement.

Together they trotted through the thicket of trees and down the hill. Aleks huffed in anger, and Christoffer let him rant. Defender ran ahead barking happily racing to sniff and mark the scents that attracted his attention. Airi flew from tree to tree, landing briefly before fluttering ahead to the next one. Skorri agitated her and Aleks alike.

"He ought to be plucked down to size," grumbled Aleks, kicking a stone out of his path.

"Plucked," agreed Airi. "Plucked, then roasted."

"'Atta girl," said Aleks. "You and Saskia always have the best ideas."

"Bloodthirsty," she chirruped.

"I bet he doesn't make for very good eating," said Christoffer, bending down to grab a large stick.

"Too scrawny," agreed Aleks. "He's not nearly so pretty as my Airi. His feathers aren't nearly as white either. Kind of grayish around the edges, don't you think?"

He shrugged. "Just around his beak and feet. His feathers are like a creamy off-white."

"He's practically yellow," said Aleks.

He wasn't, but who was Christoffer to argue? When Defender loped over, tail wagging, he threw the stick watching him run off in joy. "You got the best white raven. Isn't that right, Airi?"

"Eye-riii!" she trilled, leaping to the next tree.

Aleks nodded, kicking the stone again and stuffing his hands into his pockets. "His eyes aren't a beautiful pale blue like Airi's either. They're more like a scuzzy steel blue. Muddled."

The thicket thinned, and the hill levelled out, revealing the pond beyond. Defender dropped his stick and drank greedily at its edges, his sides panting from the playful exertion. Christoffer toe-kicked his shoes and socks off at the start of the sandy shoreline and waded into the water.

"Damn, that's cold," he said, shivering as a soft wave lapped against the back of his knees.

"You're the idiot who decided to wade in," said Aleks, unimpressed.

"Harsh, man," Christoffer complained, walking back out and plopping on the ground. The water continued to lap at his bare toes.

Aleks sat beside him, folding his legs. "Telling it like it is. You know, it's quite peaceful here. The view isn't that bad."

"Do you think it's why the Lonely One chose it for his transformation?"

Aleks scratched his neck and shrugged. "Who knows the reason. Perhaps he could see that Oskar wasn't the giant he used to be."

"So he what – spurns the rest of his kind? I don't think that's it," Christoffer said, disagreeing. With a flick of his toes, he sent the water outward in a flying arc of spray and mist. "I think his reason is simpler."

"What's your theory, then?"

Christoffer picked up a couple of flat rocks, palming them, contemplating their edges. He looked about. "I think he liked it here. It's as you said, peaceful and the view is nice. Or would be if the grass wasn't dying out in preparation for winter."

"But why here? Why not two hundred feet that way or in the opposite direction?"

"Human feet or giant feet?" He grinned and threw one of the rocks, watching it skip across the pond's surface. Four skips. Not bad.

Aleks rolled his eyes and plucked one of the stones from his hand. "What, can't you do giant to human conversions in your head?"

"Oh I can, but if I had a half of a pair of seven-league boots I'd be able to calculate faster," Christoffer joked.

Aleks threw his stone. Defender seeing it, barked and plunged into the water. He swam out to the middle of the pond and thrashed around looking for it. Laughing, Christoffer tossed another one for him, and he woofed lunging for it. His happy cavorting ended abruptly in frightened yips.

Surging to his feet, Christoffer ran into the water. "What is it, boy?"

"Airi, what do you see?" shouted Aleks, who had already shed his shoes and jacket.

She flew to the sky and circled the pond. Defender swam in jerky uncoordinated movements. The water rippled and the border collie howled, his terrified cry for help cut short, as he was yanked beneath the surface by an unseen source.

"Defender!" shouted Christoffer, diving in after him. He swam out to the middle in quick sure strokes.

"Monsters," warned Airi shrilly. "Watch out!"

A cold, scaly hand gripped Christoffer's ankle and pulled him under. He thrashed, elbowing the creature, and it let him go. In the murky gray-green gloom he spied another one holding onto his squirming, terrified dog. He swam for it, gripping its seaweed-like hair and punching it in the face. Defender broke free and swam for the surface. He pushed him upward, struggling with the dog's panic.

Before Christoffer could follow and gasp a fresh breath, he was pulled back again. A pale face with dark bulbous eyes stared at him, mouth agape and glistening like freshly spilled blood. A bobbing light flickered near its face and turned its skin a sickly pale yellow-green. He kicked at its flattened nose and pushed off, struggling for the surface as it cried in pain, surrounding him in a torrent of bubbles.

Aleks' hand plunged down to grab him, pulling him upward. Treading water, Christoffer scrubbed the droplets from his eyes and searched for his dog. Seeing him nearly to shore he sagged with relief, only to have Aleks haul him forward.

"We have to go," shouted Aleks, and Christoffer kicked hard. The two raced for the water's edge.

"They're coming, they're coming," shrieked Airi.

When one got Aleks, he nearly choked on a mouthful of water, but Christoffer kept a grip on him. Both kicking, they knocked it loose. It snarled, slinking away into the watery underworld. With one last lurch they touched the bottom of the pond, and scrambled out onto the shore, collapsing in sodden heaps, panting for air. Airi landed beside them and pecked at Aleks' sleeve.

"Dummy, dummy, dummy," she croaked in fear.

"I'm okay," he told her, pulling his cuffed wrist from her freaked tapping.

"Don't scare me again," she barked, pecking him until he rolled over and soothed her feathers.

Christoffer sat up to look for Defender only to have him appear in his face. "Ahh!" he shouted, leaning back before realizing his mistake. He looped his arms around his neck and received a lick across the chin for his efforts. "Good boy. Good boy."

They gathered their wet things, and trudged back toward the trees. Christoffer glanced behind, and the pond's surface appeared deceptively tranquil. Not a ripple crossed its surface to indicate anything had happened there. He swallowed dryly and turned again, pushing down the sense of fear.

"When we tell this to the others, we should embellish it a little, don't you think?"

"Not scary enough, was it?" asked Aleks sarcastically.

"There were hundreds swarming us. It was just you and me and a wall of claws and teeth. We barely escaped with our lives, but in the end we did, because we'd saved the mermaid princess, and her father owes us for her very life."

"The only thing true about that farce was that we barely escaped," said Aleks.

"That's the version we're telling though, unless you got one better."

"You go right on being a mermaid princess' savior. You know you'll have to marry her, right? But her dad won't let her leave to be on land, so Zaria'll have to magic you a pair of gills. You'll have to prove yourself every day as thwarted lovers seek to end your life for a chance to marry her in your place."

"Alas, mortally wounded I have to return to the surface. We'll spend the rest of our days pining for the other. It's a tragic tale of star-crossed lovers."

"You're ridiculous," Aleks chuckled as they strode back into camp looking like a pair of drenched cats.

Seeing Zaria's eyes widen in alarm, Christoffer ruffled his hair and flashed her a cheeky grin. "We went fishing –" he began to explain.

"What happened to mermaid princesses?" muttered Aleks dryly.

"Did you fall in?" asked Zaria, taking in their soaked clothes and the rivulets pooling at their feet.

"Something like that," agreed Aleks. "Think you could dry us off?"

"One Madam Brown blowout coming right up," she said. "Don't move."

Wind picked up and blew past them in a sharp cool blast. Christoffer shivered under the onslaught. "Have a care, hers were always warm."

"Oops, sorry," said Zaria, and the air warmed.

Now dry, they rejoined the group; Airi to a tree opposite Skorri. Defender, who had escaped Zaria's wind tunnel plopped into the dirt and rolled onto his side, licking his paws. Aleks searched his bag for a comb, and Christoffer rued the loss of his spikes, as his short hair fell down flat over his eyes.

"What will it take to make you leave?" Skorri grumbled, tucking his head under his wing, trying to block them out.

"Are you a raven of his word?" Henrik rejoined, as he brushed down his cloak with short brisk movements.

One steely eye appeared, glaring. "I'm not going to even dignify that with a response."

"Let's make a bet," said the Stag Lord, pausing and tilting the brush at the raven.

"A bet? What sort of bet? No, no. Better yet, why would I bet? You have nothing I want."

Henrik nodded and set aside the brush, folding the cloak before piling it carefully next to his sleeping bag. "If we lose, we will depart immediately and never bother you again. Zaria as princess of the Under Realm is a sorceress. She could enchant this land so nobody could trespass again."

Skorri perked up, lifting his head. He studied Zaria with renewed interest, before deflating. "If I lose, you want me to leave him. To return nevermore."

"Do all ravens thus quoth?" asked Christoffer, looking about and waggling his eyebrows.

"Huh?" said Geirr confused, but Zaria smiled and he was satisfied. She got his bookish reference.

"Nobody says you can't come back," said Filip. "We simply want you to meet a brownie. He's been wanting a white raven for ages."

"We freed some of your uncommunicative fellows in exchange for a meeting with you," Geirr said, leaning back on his elbows and looking up into the bowers.

"This feels like a demotion in stature," said Skorri, eyeing him suspiciously.

Christoffer mouthed at Zaria, "Pun intended?" She stifled a giggle behind her hand.

The raven kept his beady eyes on Henrik, ignoring them. "What's the bet?"

Aleks and Henrik exchanged looks. The fey king tipped his head slightly in Airi's direction and Henrik nodded. Aleks took over the negotiations. "We propose a challenge – one between you and Airi."

"No," said Skorri. "I do not need to show off."

"But –" protested Aleks only to be cut off.

"I will not leave my master's side."

"Your master wouldn't want you to be a prisoner."

Skorri barked, "I won't go. I won't. I won't."

Henrik held up his hands in surrender. "No challenges between ravens. What do you suggest?"

Skorri nibbled on a talon. He put down his foot and fluffed his feathers. "You keep from saying my master's name."

"So have you," Geirr pointed out dryly.

"It's customary among giants," Henrik explained, dropping his hands, one to rest on the pommel of his sword. "As a sign of respect. You know this."

Skorri bobbed his head and hopped down a branch. "I bet you can't find out his name."

"Ah," said Henrik, smiling broadly. "You've set before us an impossible task. You know the giants will never tell, therefore you must provide clues."

"I will, if you accept the challenge."

"We do," said Henrik, confidently.

"It's not Rumpelstiltskin is it?" asked Christoffer jokingly. "No? Just checking."

If a raven could smile, this one did. He said, "A riddle in three parts."

"Which means we get three attempts for each part," interjected Henrik.

Skorri glowered and knocked low in his throat. "First, his pets will know it, at least in part, if you're brave enough to meet them in their nests. Second, can be found in sound when one completes a true test of strength. Third is both the first and the last for a Viking oaring tradition."

"Wait, wait, wait. Did the riddles just become three impossible tasks?" Filip asked, sharing an incredulous look with Henrik. "How is this better than one?"

"It's better because it's solvable."

"If you say so, mate," Filip said dubiously.

"Fail in any part, and you forfeit the bet," warned Skorri. "When that happens, the sorceress will enact her enchantment. Then at last I will have peace."

"You probably won't accept the Lonely One either, will you?" asked Christoffer.

"Is that your final guess?" asked Skorri triumphantly.

"No!" shouted Henrik and the others.

Christoffer shied away from their glares, and Skorri pouted. It would've been funny and highly satisfying to thwart the raven, if what lay ahead wasn't so terrifying. He and Aleks had encountered the giant's pets just now by the pond. Christoffer knew the others hadn't a clue about what was in store. He locked gazes with the fey king, and the redhead's grim expression wasn't reassuring in the least.

## Chapter Eleven: Not Your Mum's Mermaids

The pond appeared darker and deeper than the Mariana Trench. That was hyperbolic, but nonetheless, Christoffer felt it appropriate. He did not relish the prospect of one of his friends going down there. They all now knew what lay beneath the placid surface. Mermaids. Creepy, scary, mermaids. Everyone's faces were grim, and he could think of nothing to lighten the mood.

Wanting to observe the proceedings, Skorri convinced Zaria to create small, contained bubbles, not unlike the larger ones Olaf used for his house. Her first few attempts had been disastrous, popping like balloons from unknown forces – perhaps the wind, or a wave, or a small insect. She glowered at the water as if it had offended her and huffed, flexing her fingers.

"Relax, you got this," Christoffer told her, squeezing her hand. "If it helps, think of it like a magic submersible instead of a bubble. Give your creations more substance."

"Those are the magic words," she said and rolled up her sleeves to try again.

"I thought it was please and thank you," he quipped.

Zaria didn't need to make a show of her magic, as it was accomplished in her thoughts. She just had to push a little mentally to bring them into reality. Magic wands, staffs, amulets, gestures, and words were totally unnecessary. It was only fear of dragons that made her keep her magic style hidden. She crept ankle-deep into the pond and sucked in a breath.

"That's bracing," she said, sucking in another breath. Before she let it out, her new bubble submersible appeared.

"Should you be doing that?" Aleks asked pointedly, flicking his gaze to Skorri.

Zaria shrugged. "I can't keep curtailing my magic; it's hampering my ability. Besides, I think Skorri –"

"Is an outsider," intoned Aleks, keeping his voice low. "We need to treat him as such. He's not staying with us, you know. He's going to Master Brown."

She blew out a breath. "You're right, of course, you're right." A second later, a grin broke out across her features. "I think, however, my magic here is done. It's staying!"

"The nests are how deep?" queried Henrik, staring down into the pond.

"Anywhere between five and fifteen meters," Skorri supplied, smirking. "You should be able to dive that, right?"

"You're sure they know the giant's name?" he pressed, untucking his shirt from his pants.

"I will not forfeit the challenge by giving bad clues."

"Not so fast, Stag Lord," Filip said, throwing out his arm to block the ellefolken prince from further unbuttoning his shirt. "If anyone is taking off their shirt around here, it's me."

With that, he dropped his arm and pulled off his T-shirt in a fluid motion. Christoffer caught Zaria eyeing her boyfriend's toned torso with interest and snickered. She blushed and mouthed a furious "What?" at him.

He quirked an eyebrow. "Oh nothing, nothing," he said, pretending to whistle and turn away.

"Remember you only get three dives or you lose. Choose wisely who will do this task." warned Skorri.

"I was born a fish," said Filip. "I'll do it."

"We're counting on you," said Henrik, redoing the buttons he'd undone. He reached into the messenger bag by his side and pulled out a little brown bottle. He handed it to Filip.

"What's this?" the green-eyed teen asked.

Suddenly sheepish, the Stag Lord cleared his throat. "It's a paste."

"Which does what?"

"Something embarrassing," Christoffer guessed, plucking the bottle and unstopping the cork to sniff its contents. His eyes watered. "Gah! What is this? It's positively pungent."

"It's better if I don't explain," he said.

"And that's supposed to help me how?" questioned Filip, sniffing the bottle curiously. His nose wrinkled in disgust as Zaria took the bottle for a whiff.

"It smells sweet to me," she said, causing Henrik to blush crimson.

Curiosity spiked, Christoffer took it back and sniffed a second time. Again, his eyes watered. "Whatever you're smelling, Princess, we're not."

"Give me that," huffed Henrik, snatching back the bottle. He thrust it at Filip. "Look it's not meant to be mixed with water."

Filip eyed the pond around him and quirked an eyebrow. "Okay, mate."

He rolled his eyes. "It turns into a sticky slime when it does. Use it on the mermaids. Cover their gills and they'll leave you alone."

Zaria gasped. "That'll kill them!"

"Maybe," Henrik agreed. "More likely it'll break down and dissolve before that time comes. The mermaids will be trying to scrape it off, too."

"Thanks," said Filip, tucking the bottle into his pocket. He turned to Zaria and held out a hand. "Kiss for luck?"

She took it, but instead of stepping back onto the shoreline she tugged him to her and tilted her face up to his. They kissed and Christoffer felt a moment of envy, not for the girl, but because there was one. Luckily for them all Skorri broke them apart before it went beyond PG-13. The white raven clipped Filip's temple and landed in the crown of Zaria's hair.

"Enough sucking face," he grumped. "Are you diving, human? Or not?"

"Someone's got his tail feathers in a knot," Christoffer chortled, refusing to shrink under the raven's narrowed regard.

"Be safe," Zaria whispered, bussing her boyfriend's cheek. "I'll be watching."

"I won't be in any danger, Zar-Zar. I have you," he said, tucking a loose strand of hair behind her ear.

"Daylight's fading," warned Airi.

The midnight sun would prevent true darkness, but the crepuscular light would linger with ever lengthening purple shadows from the giant's lone form. The wind picked up, gently stirring the pond's surface. Nearby insects droned in the tall, yellow grass. Nothing spoke of danger, and yet, all were aware of it lurking nearby.

Zaria herded everyone into her transparent, plastic-like submersible. Christoffer grasped the edge of the hatch to hoist himself inside. At the water line, inside the bubble, a circular bench ran around the entire circumference. It felt like sitting in an invisible car. He could see himself, and kept waiting to get wet, but it never happened. The submersible seemed to disappear, but he knew that was only an illusion.

Patting the seat appreciatively, Christoffer whistled. "Wicked."

"Best seats in the house for everyone," Zaria said with pride as she stepped inside and closed the hatch, twisting it into place. She settled beside Christoffer and held his hand tightly, watching as Filip dunked himself fully to get used to the temperature. "Mermaids, you say?"

"Mermaids," he said. "Not your mum's mermaids either. These things are like horrors from the deep. Think mermaid versions of Igor and Gollum combined."

Even though her eyes clouded with worry, she tried to inject a little levity. "Did you know that Igor wasn't in Mary Shelley's novel?"

"Once a bookworm, always a bookworm."

"You say that like it's a bad thing," she said with a moue, but there was no sting in her words.

He slung an arm around her shoulders. "Never. The more reading you do, the less I have to do."

She laughed and pushed him away. "That's not how it works, you know."

"It isn't?" he said with fake surprise. "Well, damn."

Through the bubble they saw Filip give them a thumbs up and begin the challenge by diving from the shallows and sinking beneath the waves. They watched in silence – Zaria lowering the submersible alongside him. As he sank beneath the waves, so, too, did they. The murky gloom glowed eerily, as light diffused in even layers before petering out in the center of the lake where the depths awaited.

A school of silver fish darted forward and away as Filip followed the slanting slope of the bed. Using vegetation to pull himself along, he steadily progressed toward the center of the pond until it fell away revealing a gorge so black it felt like looking into starless sky. Bubbles trickled slowly from his nose as he tilted himself down and launched himself off the ledge. He swam with fluid movements, looking indeed like the fish he proclaimed to be.

Tension mounted in the bubble, as darkness bled into the scene like ink. Shadows moved in time, it seemed with their breaths, so Christoffer held his. Something sluiced past them, causing Zaria and Geirr to shriek and cling to their neighbors. Henrik gently pried Geirr off him, while Christoffer ran a soothing hand along Zaria's back.

"What was that?" asked Henrik. "Was that what I think it was?"

"It was," said Aleks grimly. "Nothing else that big would be in the pond."

"Is he in danger?" Zaria asked, looking over her shoulder at him, as she pressed her hand against the bubble's side in quiet worry.

"How many are there?" asked Geirr, not for the first time.

"My master never kept a census," Skorri said dismissively.

"It's circling," Airi croaked, making a warning knocking sound deep in her throat.

"I don't like this," said Geirr, cringing back into his collar.

The shadow attacked. There was no sound even though two musical notes looped endlessly inside Christoffer's head in ever increasing frequency. Zaria held still, poised for action, nearly vibrating in her need to lend a hand, but with the mermaid locked in a spirally death match with Filip she had no clear shot.

Light glinted faintly off a flurry of bubbles when, as suddenly as the attack started, it stopped. The shadow flew back in one direction, and Filip in the other. He kicked hard for the surface, reaching desperately for its glimmering edge, as if it were something tangible he could cling to and haul himself up with.

Purple light engulfed him and flew him upwards as the bubble raced along behind. They breeched the surface at the same time, Filip gasping for breath. He swam toward the shoreline, something white and translucent like seafoam clutched in his fist. He waded to the beach and tossed it on the ground as Zaria opened the hatch. Skorri flew up beside her and perched on its edge.

"What do you have there?" he clucked.

Filip grimaced, hands on knees, as he sucked in air. "I think it's skin."

"Did I hear you right? You tore its skin off?" Aleks asked from inside the bubble.

"Gross," said Airi, ruffling her feathers.

Henrik shook his head. "Not really. They slough their skin like a snake to allow for growth. Filip must have encountered one in the middle of the process."

"Do you have your answer?" asked Skorri, eyeing Filip's shivering form with disdain.

He shook his head. "I'm going back down."

"Are you sure?" Zaria asked, concern etched across her face and in her violet eyes.

He dipped his body below the water, up to his neck, and nodded. "I'm not sure what we're looking for, but I don't think that's it. Do you think you could give me some light to see by when we're down there?"

She nodded. "Of course. I should have done it before. I didn't think. Are you warm enough?"

"I'll be warmer once I get moving."

She bit her lip, but smiled and let it go when he blew her a kiss. As he took off, she dipped back inside the submersible. Skorri followed suit, and the hatch was closed and locked, reforming the airtight seal. The descent this time went at a fast clip, as Filip wasted no time in reaching the underwater cliff.

He plunged over its edge, and as he dove, a hazy purple light began to glow around his body. Curious fish swam toward him only to dart and swerve as they recognized the danger. Another sloping floor greeted them, and at the base, glittering lights reflected along the cliff's edge.

"Do you think that's more of the ore like in Malmdor?" Christoffer asked, trying to peer closer. "Is the purple from it or from you, Zaria?"

"Those are the nests," Henrik warned, his mouth thinning, as his eyebrows drew down sharply.

Filip must have noticed that, too, and swam closer. Zaria's nails bit into Christoffer's arm, and he had to pry them off one finger at a time. He made a joke, but no one seemed to hear, or if they did, they ignored it. Poor timing.

"That isn't ore," shouted Aleks, lurching from the other side of the bubble and sending them tumbling, as the submersible careened forward.

The ravens screeched and flapped their wings, sending feathers everywhere in the confusion of the next few moments. Someone cried in pain as talons scraped skin raw. Christoffer landed on top of Zaria through no fault of his own, as they went end over end. She wheezed dazedly under him. He scrambled off her, pulled mentally in two directions – one to help her and two to find Filip. He realized the blind panic he was in wasn't him at all. Zaria's light had winked out.

"I can't see him," said Aleks.

Fulminating, Geirr hissed, "If you had just stayed in your seat, we'd know what's going on out there."

"What did you see?" asked Henrik.

"You okay, Zaria?" asked Christoffer. He crouched slowly and waved his arms in big swooping arcs until he found her. "Come on, get up."

She inhaled and light suddenly returned to the world like a flame. It illuminated a thrilling scene like out of a horror movie. The glittering lights along the base of the cliff were starkly revealed and they were not, as Christoffer once thought, the glow of the purple ore that lined the halls of Malmdor. No, as Aleks had seen, those lights were attached to something more menacing than scenery.

Mermaids swarmed around Filip, eager to feast and feed. They snapped and snarled at one another, fighting for the right to claim him as a meal. With his blade unsheathed, Filip brandished it at the nearest one, while struggling to escape the clasp of another latched on his ankle. Sharp, irregular-sized teeth too long and large for the mouth which contained them, opened wide. Before the mermaid could latch onto his leg Zaria flung the bubble toward the mob forcing them to scatter or be blasted into the wall.

Filip latched onto the hatch's handle and let Zaria fly them upwards to the surface. This time their friend did not make for the shoreline. He waited for Zaria to fling the hatch wide and lifted his sword to her. On its end was another crumpled sheath of skin. It looked similar to the wrapper of a straw when accordion folded and made to grow with water. She handed it down to Geirr, who took it with distaste.

"Thanks for the assist, Zar-Zar," Filip wheezed.

"You're not hurt, are you?" she asked, clasping his hand tightly.

"Right as rain," he assured her through blue-tinged lips.

"Do you have your answer?" asked Skorri.

He pushed his wet hair off his forehead. "I have one last dive, and I intend to use it."

Zaria protested, "It's too dangerous."

"I can do it, Zar-Zar."

Filip surged upward and kissed her startled mouth before dropping like a stone into the water. With a deep breath, he plunged beneath the waves. Zaria scrambled to pull down the hatch and follow suit. As she passed him, he latched onto the hatch again and let the submersible suck him down into the darkened depths.

Christoffer pointed to the skin in Geirr's hands. "Can I see that?"

"Take it," he said and passed it over gladly.

Examining it, Christoffer found that the sloughed skin held impressions of scales. Detailed in dots and stripes the sheath became something fascinating and strange as he tried to perceive a pattern. Under his fingertips, it felt like wax paper and clung to his skin.

The weakest spot seemed to be the middle where it was stretched thin like cheese cloth. He wasn't afraid of ripping it by mistake, for it held too much strength in its fibers. Clinging to one of the scales was a bone white bead on a thread of seaweed. He plucked it off and held it aloft. On it was a trace of lettering, but nothing he could discern.

"For me?" asked Airi with an avaricious gleam.

He tucked it into his pocket with a shake of his head. "Maybe later."

"He's going to search a nest," Geirr groaned, running a hand down his face. "That's the worst move he could make. A mermaid's going to pop out and eat him. I can't watch this."

"Shh," hushed Zaria, scanning the blackness for signs of movement.

Christoffer saw the mermaid appear like a mare behind Filip. It loomed over him, dark stringy hair floating out behind it like the tentacles of a squid. It reached for him with ghostly thin fingers, stretching its joints into claws. Filip spun around, catching it in the act and thrust his hands out, grabbing its face. The mermaid clawed at his hands in desperation. Wresting himself away, he watched as the mermaid retreated, frantically trying to clear its gills from Henrik's slimy paste.

Seeing his chance, Filip shot up in a blaze of bubbles. Zaria was quick to boost him up, catching him and pushing him upward with the submersible. All the while Skorri made pleased knocking sounds.

"No more dives," he trilled. "You should have sent someone else in his place."

"Don't count your spells before they're cast," said Zaria sharply, violet eyes flashing.

When they made it to shore, she was the first out and by Filip's side. He shook all over, teeth chattering from the cold, and blue around his extremities. Zaria hit him with a blast of hot air, and kept it on him long after he dried, until he begged her to stop, his face red from her efforts, as heat blazed his cheeks. Satisfied that he wouldn't succumb to hypothermia she crushed her mouth to his and gave him another layer of warmth.

"Did you find anything?" asked Henrik, when they parted. He focused on collecting the skins from Christoffer and the ground.

Filip cleared his throat and held out a tiny bead. "I only found this."

"For me? For me?" begged Airi.

"No girl," said Aleks. "Not this time."

"Do you have your answer?" queried Skorri.

Henrik stared coolly at the white raven. "You said the mermaids held the answer but only in part."

Christoffer gathered the bead from Filip and peered at it closely. It too held faint markings. He shook his head, his next words causing Filip to slump in defeat. "It's not legible."

"Then we're not guessing yet," Henrik told Skorri, who harrumphed and took flight.

Glancing down at them from under his wing, he shouted, "You won't win. You won't win."

Yawning to relieve his ears from pressure, Christoffer wiggled a finger in one. Softly taunting, he said, "Is somebody talking? I can't hear anything."

# Chapter Twelve: A Strongman's Competition

By unanimous consent, the group decided to settle in for the night instead of seeking the next task. Scuppered, Skorri sulked all night, settling some distance from them, nesting high on the transformed giant's head. The more Christoffer saw of the raven, the more he felt a match with Master Brown would work out swimmingly. He could just imagine the two getting along like Statler and Waldorf from that old kid's series on television, *The Muppet Show*, well-suited for their malcontent dispositions and all around curmudgeonliness.

It was the general opinion of everyone that Airi was the superior raven, even if her vocabulary was somewhat limited. Whether Skorri's loquaciousness was a result of time or environment or master nobody knew, not even Henrik, although he suspected it might be a little of column A and a little of column B and a little of column C. When pressed for the third time, Christoffer agreed with Aleks over dinner preparations that she would surpass the male in her command of lexicon and language.

"You're haranguing me like an old woman," Christoffer complained, when Aleks tried to bring it up for the fourth time. He angled the prep knife at him. "I know he got under your skin, but you're giving him too much power."

Aleks frowned grumpily, but slowly closed his mouth and nodded. He sighed, "You're right. I know you are, but — nobody, nobody, messes with my girl and gets away with it. Even if he's a feathered nitwit."

"Especially if he's a feathered nitwit," he teased.

"If he hurts her feelings, I'll pluck out all his plumage and stuff a pillow with it."

Christoffer chuckled. "I think Saskia and Airi are rubbing off on you. That was particularly violent."

Aleks turned sheepish. "I'm a little overprotective."

He shrugged and scraped the chopped vegetables into the pan, covering them with foil. "Hey, man, if Saskia doesn't complain who am I to do so?"

"Oh, she'd complain," Aleks said dryly, offering a wry smile. He finished prepping the rabbits Henrik snared earlier and placed them over the campfire.

"You could hold your own. That girl is just as overprotective of you. She might not like it, but she'd see it was a fair turnabout."

Zaria joined them, undoing her braids as she sat on a log next to them. Her long brown hair curled in tight waves down her back. "I can't wait to eat that."

Christoffer grinned. "I bet it tastes all the sweeter because you didn't have to conjure it."

She laughed. "You bet it does."

"How's Filip doing?" asked Aleks.

"He's asleep; poor thing just crashed."

"What! Without food?" gasped Christoffer. "Are we in a parallel dimension? Has the world ended?"

"Be nice," said Zaria, just as Aleks said, "Ye of little faith. He'll wake when the smell of meat reaches him. You just wait and see if he doesn't."

"Oh, good," Christoffer said, with a fake sigh of relief. "I was worried we had already been consumed by the dragon and were lost forever."

Zaria pushed him. "He's not that bad about food. He's not any worse than the lot of you."

"I'm wounded," he pouted. "I work hard to maintain this manly physique. It requires diligence, a balanced diet, and daily exercise regimes."

She raised an eyebrow and held out her hands.

"Ooo, look. Cake!" Christoffer said happily, snatching a slice from her conjured offerings.

"You were saying?"

"Okay, okay. You win," he said, words muffled by sugary goodness.

They dissolved into laughter, and the evening turned into all things sweet and happy. As predicted, Filip was awakened by the aroma of roasted rabbit. He appeared bleary eyed in their midst, and everyone cheered his successful dives. He beamed bashfully under the praise.

They ate dinner, taking time to pass around the beads. Everyone took a turn and raised each bead to the light to peer closely at its surface. They ran their thumbs over the raised edges looking for openings and searching for hidden messages. If anything had been inscribed, it was now illegible. They had all confirmed it. The beads appeared to be utterly useless. Filip took it harder than the others, his disheartened expression sinking even lower.

Zaria soothingly ran her hand along his back and kissed his temple. "There must be a secret or a trick we've yet to discover. We'll keep working on it. You did your part. You did the impossible. I'm so, so incredibly proud of you."

"I love you, Zar-Zar," he whispered, touching his forehead to hers.

Her eyes softened, and she took him gently by his hand and led him away from the others. Christoffer watched them go and let out a cat call, laughing riotously when Filip flipped him off. Waggling his eyebrows at Geirr, he plucked a piece of meat from the rabbit and ate it. When the blue-eyed teen ignored him, he looked to Henrik for comradery.

"We bachelors need to stick together, am I right?"

"Hey!" complained Aleks. "I'm still here."

Geirr rolled his eyes and tore a hunk of meat for himself. "What's your point? You're just as besotted as our friend Filip."

Aleks brushed back his bangs and grabbed for another helping. He pointed a leg at them. "I disagree with your terminology."

"You would," said Christoffer, laughing.

Geirr raised his eyebrows. "If your future queen was here, would you still be sitting with us?"

"If our positions were reversed –" sputtered Aleks.

"They're not, but I get your point."

"You can be an honorary bachelor tonight," Christoffer offered magnanimously.

"I'm going to bed," Aleks said with a huff, calling an end to the ribbing.

Henrik concurred, looking upset and murmuring, "I need to prepare for tomorrow's challenge."

"You all right?" asked Christoffer. "How's that unrequited love?"

"He doesn't want to talk about it," said Geirr, frowning harshly.

Henrik shrugged. "It's okay, Geirr. All I can say is that I'm better than yesterday and the day before that and the one before that. They're good together."

"They are," Christoffer agreed. "Okay. Well, when you're ready, just say the word; I'll plan a guys' night. We'll go all out and paint the town red."

"I'm in," said Geirr, collecting the dirty dishes.

Christoffer looped his arms around both their necks. "Excellent! Now we just need to get this dragon business behind us."

Aleks yawned and banked the fire. "For all his talk of game, I bet ten to one Christoffer is the first married out of all of us."

Geirr thought about it and held out his hand. "I'll take that bet. It's going to be you."

"You might be right," he said, clasping hands. "I can afford to be wrong."

They walked to where the tents huddled next to the base of the Lonely One, using the transformed giant as a shield from the wind. Aleks stopped to dig into his bag for a change of clothes and his toothbrush. From the other tent whispers and murmurs could be heard, though lights were out.

"Goodnight lovebirds," cooed Christoffer to the occupied tent, and their whispering stopped.

"Is it safe?" muttered Geirr. "Should I move my things?"

The zipper slid down and Zaria stuck her head out. "That depends," she said.

"On what?"

"On if you plan to be smart with me," she said, but her eyes were not on him.

While Christoffer clutched his heart in faux wounded outrage, Geirr made a locking motion across his mouth and pretended to throw away the key. "I'll behave."

"I believe you. I don't believe him."

This caused everyone to laugh.

The next morning the group followed the floating pair of white ravens. They rode a warm thermal across the plains leading to a low-lying field, invisible to the naked eye until they were practically on top of it. Defender barked happily and raced to sniff it all.

Glacial erratic littered the valley. Some of the stones were bigger than tiny houses; others, like tree stumps. More were considerably smaller, like bowling balls. Ten pillars vaguely resembling fingers stood in the center of the field. As they got closer, Christoffer saw they even had indentations like nailbeds. Had all this once been a giant?

It would be the Stag Lord's task to sift and sort the stones, then lift ten of them one at a time onto the top of the pillars. Skorri wanted the glacial dropstones sorted by size, with the heaviest ones in the middle. The pillars in the middle were the tallest ones, which meant that Henrik had a more difficult challenge twice over with the final two boulders. The white raven wanted him to fail, that much was clear.

"You may begin your challenge," said Skorri, swooping down and claiming the tiny-house-sized rock for his outlook.

Airi tried to perch next to Skorri but he scared her off. She screeched in anger and made a beeline for Aleks. Settling on his leather-clad shoulder, she croaked, "Boorish toad."

"Harpy," retorted Skorri.

Eyeing the pile of rocks before Henrik, Geirr asked, "Does this remind you of your summers with the witch?"

Filip toed one the size of a small baseball and whistled, surprised at how resistant it was. "Nobody else is built for this, mate. It has to be you, Henrik."

"Hey, it's just lifting rocks. I could probably do it," Christoffer said cockily, swaggering over.

Bending to pick up one of the stony bowling balls, Christoffer grunted and nearly flattened himself. The rock, much heavier than it looked, didn't budge. He made a grab for it with both hands and lifted it to his lap, groaning the whole way. When he couldn't get a better grip, he let go and it fell with a loud clatter to the ground. He cautiously prodded another, larger one, and couldn't move it at all.

"All right, so maybe not," he conceded to Geirr's and Filip's knowing looks. "Lifting these is going to be way harder than it looks."

Henrik continued to assess the stones and nodded gravely. "This is not going to be pleasant."

He removed his golden-antlered cloak, folded it carefully, and placed it beside his bag. He wore a graphic tee, stretched tight across his chest, and a pair of gym shorts underneath. The cool wind caused gooseflesh to rise on his arms, but he paid it no heed.

From his bag he took out a roll of athletic tape and placed it on top. He took time limbering up, stretching out ligaments and loosening joints. Only after stretching did he spend time taping up his forearms, prepping for the lifts to come. When he was ready, he faced the pillars.

Pretending to be a coach, Christoffer rubbed Henrik's shoulders. "Okay, Champ. This here today is what you've been training for all your life. You've given your time, your energy, your strength, and your sweat. Now is the time to give it more. Give it your all!"

"Which are you going to move first?" asked Zaria. "Will you do the heavier ones to get those out of the way? Or the smaller ones to get as many done as soon as possible?"

"I'm going to work outside to inside," said Henrik. "I have to save those big ones for last, or I'll be worn out before I get a chance to do the others."

"Just be careful," she cautioned. "It's not worth an injury. We can find another way."

"Filip bearded the mermaids in their nests. I can do this," Henrik assured her, brushing back his bangs.

Aleks linked an arm around her shoulders and pulled her back. "He'll be fine, none of the rocks have teeth."

"How do you know?" asked Christoffer. "You don't know these rocks. They may, too, have teeth."

"Don't go inviting trouble," warned Geirr.

"The last thing we need is rocks with teeth, mate," agreed Filip. "Hazardous mermaids were enough, thank you very much."

Christoffer shrugged and folded himself up on the ground, welcoming Defender who'd come trotting back from marking everything in the field. "What can I say? Everybody lacks imagination."

"I think we need to knock everything over," said Aleks eyeing the pile. "You don't want to lift and place something up there only to have to do it again, if there's a larger or smaller stone later."

"You're right," agreed Henrik as he put all his weight against the middle section, leaning in. Aleks and Filip joined him and together they toppled the pile of rocks to the ground.

Everyone spent a moment surveying the lot, organizing them visually. There were two roughly a foot long, and a third that looked like it might be in the same category, but was hard to judge by appearance. One was nearly spherical like a beach ball, which had been hiding behind one which was shaped similarly, but with more irregularities.

Another rock with a hole in the center looked somewhat like a tire and also contained a few surprises. It held two smaller stones. Then there were two cubical stones, flat and smooth on the edges. The remaining two were oddly shaped, but were more round than not, and would probably take a crane to lift. All counted, that meant there were twelve rocks and ten pillars. Henrik would have to choose the right ten to win.

"That's lucky," said Henrik.

"Lucky? Your definition of lucky and mine are not the same," said Christoffer. "You'd have to be a beast to lift all these."

"Lucky, because the ones I have to guess at are on the smaller end of the scale. It'll be a little annoying but not impossible."

"What can we do to help?" asked Zaria.

Henrik looked at Skorri. "Are they allowed to help me set up?"

The white raven honked in laughter.

"We'll take that as a 'no' then," said Geirr.

Henrik stooped to pick up the first stone. It lifted easily and he toted it to the first pillar on the left. He proceeded to do the same with two more of the smallest ones, alternating right and left. By the end, he was perspiring heavily along his temples and had to wipe his face with his shirt.

"How much do you figure those weighed?" asked Christoffer, looking at Filip.

"Somewhere between one and two Defenders."

"Useless," said Airi.

"What was that, girl?" asked Aleks.

"Useless. Useless," she said hopping up and down.

"O—kay," said Aleks, drawing out the syllables. "Well, this next one he would be doing has got to be –"

"Weakling," squawked Airi.

"Wow, harsh much?" said Christoffer. "You know he's on our side, right? You should be encouraging him, not tearing him down."

"Stones, dummy," she chirruped. "Three weakling."

"Do you understand what she's saying?" asked Geirr.

Aleks scratched his neck and shrugged. "I think she's classifying the stones by their weight."

"Yes, weight," she agreed, nipping his ear affectionately.

Henrik grunted and lifted another stone onto his shoulders, let it rest, and walked to its pillar. With this stone, he had landed six. Sweat plastered his shirt to his back and chest. Zaria handed him a towel and a thermos of cool water, which he took gratefully.

He looped the stone with the hole next and hefted it to the first of the middle pillars. He rolled it up and settled it in place with a grunt before squaring off to the third to last rock. Sweat from the effort poured off him like a river. Standing, Henrik pulled the clinging shirt over his head and tossed it behind him.

He swept his slick bangs off his forehead and cast Filip an arched look, daring him to complain. He frowned, but said nothing. The blond teen was built like a swimmer; Henrik was built like a strongman. His shoulders, chest, and back were heavily defined.

"He looks like the Mountain's younger brother," said Geirr with a low whistle.

"It's no wonder he can power lift like he does," agreed Aleks. "Maybe I should've spent my summers with the witch."

"You still could," Henrik said jokingly, drying himself off, and peeling away the wet tape.

He spent the time to rewrap his arms. Doing so also allowed him to recoup some of his energies and to catch his breath. Still, he gave a heavy sigh, when he moved to take on the remaining stones.

"Last half-strength," Airi said as Henrik positioned himself to the larger of the cubical stones and lapped it. With an explosive thrust from his hips, Henrik got it to chest height and carried it to its home.

"Two left," he told them, coming to stand behind the second largest stone.

"You're tired. Take a rest. Have something to eat and drink," said Zaria, gesturing toward the ground where a blanket and spread appeared at her command.

Defender took immediate notice and woofed, heading for the food. Three people spoke at once:

Christoffer blocked his dog with a firm, "No."

Henrik shook his head and said, "I'll eat when I'm done."

And loudest of all, Skorri said, "No breaks allowed."

Filip reached for a stem of grapes and plucked off a handful. Using them to give a mock toast, he said, "We'll let the feast celebrate your victory."

Wedging his fingers under the boulder, Henrik heaved. Pressing it to his chest and wrapping his arms tightly around it, he got it into position. Staggering slightly under its weight, he walked to the pillar on the right and leaned back, lifting with his hips and arms and shoulders, using all his might.

"Arrgh," he shouted, carrying it over.

Stumbling over a thick stone, he pitched forward and dropped it. Luckily, Zaria was fast on her magic and conjured a mattress to cushion his fall. He flopped onto it, winded, but otherwise unhurt.

Picking himself up, Henrik gingerly approached the rock now resting at the base of the pillar. Geirr and Aleks kicked at nearby rocks to get them out of his path. Dropping into position, Henrik lapped the rock and heaved with all his might. The rock went up, up, and into its cradle. Resting his forehead against the stony column, he sucked in great gulps of air.

"Last one," hooted Skorri. He turned and scratched at his tail feathers. "You won't make it."

"I'll make it," Henrik swore, his blue eyes flashing.

"Nobody's ever finished all seventeen hundred pounds on this course."

"Watch me," the Stag Lord said, lifting his head and raising his chin.

"Wait, just how many fools have tried to sort these rocks?" questioned Christoffer, to no answer.

"Well then, go on. What are you waiting for?" mocked the raven.

"I could happily pluck that pigeon and cook his goose," growled Zaria, plopping herself down on the blanket beside Filip.

Christoffer laughed, "Man, everybody has it out for his plumage."

Filip brushed a kiss by her ear. "Just remember, we need him to get the you-know-what fixed."

Christoffer settled onto the blanket and ate a grape. "If anyone can beat the raven at this game, it will be Henrik, don't you worry. The ancient Egyptians couldn't haul stone like he hauls it."

"I don't think it was the Egyptians doing the hauling," Zaria replied, handing him a plate.

Despite looking like he had run out of steam, Henrik lined up to the last stone. Reaching straight down, he wedged the stone between his elbows and forearms. Gritting his teeth, he angled his hands deep under the stone, letting its weight settle. With a full deep breath he braced himself, and after a small hesitation, exploded upwards. Arms and legs trembling like jello, he walked it to the waiting platform.

Carefully, he brought his feet together, and leaning back, rolled the rock upwards against his torso. As he went to get a better grip, the stone slipped. They all gasped in horror, and Christoffer nearly choked on a grape. Henrik, swiftly shifting positions and dropping into a squat, managed to save his toes from a terrible fate. Breathing hard he set the rock down and stood, wiping his brow.

"You're so close," cheered Zaria, raising clenched fists in the air.

"One last lift, and then you forfeit," Skorri warned.

"How do you reckon that?" asked Filip, frowning.

Christoffer came up beside him and shaded his eyes. "He reset twice. If he fails to load the stone on his next attempt, then his three chances are up."

"He'll load it," said Geirr confidently.

"Thanks, everyone," said Henrik wearily, nearly wilting on his feet, all reserves spent.

With grim determination, and pure grit, he straddled the stone and hunkered down. Despite his fatigue, he looked ready to do battle. Working himself into position, he hugged the rock hard into his body, inhaled, and with an upward blast of movement extended his reach until the stone rested just on the lip of the platform.

"Errrrr!" he yelled, quivering with effort.

He pushed it up, up, up… and teetered on total collapse, but in the final trembling moments – it was like a cinematic experience – sound faded, time held still, and with a soft breath of wind, gravity took over and pulled the stone into its housing. Only then did Henrik collapse, hands on knees, his body juddering with shaky breath.

# Chapter Thirteen: Not the Final Guess

Christoffer whooped and leapt off the ground, racing to his exhausted friend. Tackling him, he shouted, "I knew you had this in the bag!"

Straightening, Henrik inhaled deeply through his nose, before letting his breath out slowly through his mouth. "I don't think I could have done it without everyone's support. Knowing you were all on my side was the push I needed to get through those last two loads."

"Lunch," stated Zaria firmly, directing him to his place. "You need to refuel."

Wobbling on his feet, and looking like a feather could knock him over, Henrik made his way to the blanket. There, slowly folding in on himself, he sat down and then flopped like the strings had been cut. He sprawled and stretched out on the ground, easing out kinked muscles and tight ligaments. His eyes drifted closed and his words slurred, "Maybe a quick nap, first."

As the Stag Lord slept, the others parsed out his performance looking for the solution to Skorri's riddle while eating from the various dishes Zaria had created. Everyone had a guess as to what sound a strongman would make, but as Christoffer pointed out there were really only two options, for both sounds occurred when Henrik dealt with the heaviest of the boulders.

"So we agree, it's either '*ar*' or '*er,*'" he said, closing one eye and brandishing an imaginary weapon. "Like a pirate. Do we know any pirate names?"

"Blackbeard," suggested Geirr.

"Bluebeard," offered Filip.

Aleks grinned, pointing to his hair, "Or Redbeard."

"Long John Silver or Jack Sparrow," Zaria added.

Christoffer pulled a face. Teasing he said, "Those aren't going to work at all. Greybeard at least fits the facial hair theme."

"Forkbeard," croaked Airi.

"See, she gets it," he said, tipping an imaginary hat in the raven's direction. Airi preened under the praise.

"Alas, I can never live up to that moniker," mourned Aleks rubbing his chin. "That ship has sailed."

Zaria rolled her eyes. "All right, fine. Moving on, what about the beads?"

They were no closer to a solution there. The beads passed from hand to hand, as their friend woke from his nap and stretched his sore muscles. Henrik joined them and ate a late repast. He, too, took his time examining the beads under the light of day and frowned at their rather unremarkable appearance.

"What are we missing?" he asked the group at large.

"That's what I'd like to know," agreed Christoffer.

"Are we focusing on the wrong thing? What if it's not the beads at all, but the skins?" asked Filip, standing up and going to Henrik's bag. "May I?"

Henrik nodded. "Help yourself. The skins are in there, tucked away at the bottom."

Filip dug to the bottom of the bag and pulled them out. Pond smells wafted up like floating seaweed, subtle and soft. He laid them on the ground, smoothing out their creases. His friend moved to straighten out the tail of one and spied another bead. He leaned forward and snatched it up triumphantly.

"Here's another for our collection."

Eager hands reached out; each wanting to be the one to discover and reveal its secret. Geirr got the bead first and held it up to his nose, squinting. Seeing nothing he shrugged and held it out for the others. The erosion on the bead matched the other two they found. Little, nonsensical, raised stripes dotted its surface like Morse Code made into Braille.

The discarded waxy skin gleamed dully in the sunlight giving off an appearance of antique paper. Its cousin lay equally ignored nearby. Striations in the scales revealed where the mermaid had encountered Filip's short sword and where he had hooked the sloughing skin.

Aleks ran his fingers over the rough tear, poking a finger through to the other side and testing the texture. When he flipped it over to reveal the brighter side, a small object pinged against the ground. He bent to pick it up, adding a fourth bone-white bead to their growing collection.

"This one is newer than the others," he said excitedly. "I can see shapes on it. Does it look like triangular infinity sign to you?"

"Rune," said Airi, peering over his shoulder.

Henrik held out his hand and Aleks gave him the bead to examine. "The rune is dagaz. Its literal translation is day or dawn."

"Two triangles?" asked Zaria, looking at one of the earlier beads. She squinted. "I think that's what's here, but part of it is rubbed smooth."

"Same for this one," agreed Filip, looking between her bead and his. "I appear to have some of the parts missing from Zaria's."

"Now we're getting somewhere," Christoffer crowed. "The giant's name is Day-arrr!"

Skorri clicked his beak excitedly. "Is that –"

"No!" everyone retorted, shooting Christoffer a quelling glare.

He held up his hands in surrender. "Am I not allowed to spitball? How else are we supposed to come up with the answer? Aren't we brainstorming?"

"We are," agreed Zaria. She shot a furious look at Skorri and wagged her finger at him. "Until we tell you otherwise, we are not presenting our final answer to the riddle."

Skorri scowled, fluffing his feathers and scratching at his neck in agitation. Dropping his talon, he preceded to ignore them with a huffed, "Fine."

"Remember, Christoffer, there's more to this," cautioned Henrik, collecting all four beads; presenting them in his palm. He picked them up one by one as he spoke. "We're working on a compound riddle. The parts can be either words, syllables, or letters. We'll need to solve all three parts to get the clues to solve the Lonely One's name."

"We've solved two, can't we extrapolate?" he whined.

"As long as you realize your guesses are at best incomplete and at worst focusing on the wrong aspect of the proffered clue."

Aleks leaned forward, elbows on knees and steepled his fingers. "The last challenge is a traditional Viking oaring challenge, whatever that is, but that small issue aside, I must point out, we lack a longboat and oars."

"If only we knew a sorceress," Zaria teased, touching a finger to her chin pretending to think hard. "Who do we know that could introduce us to one?"

"Oh, I don't know," said Christoffer. "One might just appear when we need her most."

"There's an easier, less magical way to procure what we need," said Geirr. "Isn't Bjarke coming today? Why don't we send him a message?"

"I deliver," said Airi at once, with a little hopping step so she faced him.

Aleks nodded. "Find him and tell him that we need his and his crew's talents for a challenge."

"King Aleks need Bjarke," she repeated, and after an affectionate nip to his fingers, took flight.

Skorri watched her go, and Christoffer thought he detected a hint of envy in the raven's gaze. It appeared that someone missed being a messenger and flying off to meet new people and places. The lure might be enough to sway the raven, even if they were unable to solve the riddle. Although with the way they were crushing these challenges, Christoffer had a feeling they'd solve it, and while he still liked his guess of Dayar for the Lonely One, he agreed with the others that it probably wasn't the final choice.

"You know, if I had sent the message, it wouldn't have been shortened," Skorri said nonchalantly, nibbling on a talon.

Knowing his friend's penchant for angry defense of his pet, Christoffer spoke before Aleks could. After all, they were not trying to rile the white raven, if they could help it. At least that's what everyone kept telling him. "You are exceptionally gifted. Did you practice? Is it a memorization skill?"

"Yes," said Skorri, setting his foot down and peering at him. "With a giant like mine for a master, one must honor his words. He spoke so infrequently and with such deliberation that to forget one was a serious breach of translation and a dereliction of duties."

"Airi's not –" Aleks began.

"You must've practiced very diligently," said Christoffer, standing on Aleks' foot, causing the redhead to curse under his breath. "I'm impressed that you know as many words as you do if the giant spoke so infrequently."

"My Du –"

"Yes?" he pressed, hoping to trick the raven and gain the giant's full name.

Skorri clicked his beak, and started over. "My duties synced with my master's hobbies. He liked to read, and he loved music. Between books and songs I had a thorough training."

Disappointed, Christoffer deflated. 'Du' wasn't the first part of the giant's name at all, then. Just the first syllable in duties.

"You might want to introduce both to Airi, Aleks," Zaria said, packing up the remnants from lunch.

Defender gazed at her adoringly, placing a paw on her knee. Succumbing to his doleful eyes, she passed him a few scraps, earning his love forever. He licked her hand after he'd woofed it down.

The redheaded teen looked like he wanted to protest, but swallowed and nodded. "I just might. Not because she's lacking in any way, mind you, but because she might enjoy both. I wouldn't want to deprive her of anything that would make her happy."

Filip folded the blanket and tucked it under his arm. "We should head back to the coast. If Airi brings Bjarke to us, we should be there to meet him."

They all agreed and collected their belongings. Skorri took to the air, as Filip helped Zaria, taking what she had, so she wasn't burdened. Aleks and Geirr slung their bags over their shoulders, while Henrik donned his cloak. Of course, he hadn't brought anything but himself and his dog, so Christoffer was unencumbered as well. Whistling for Defender's attention, he called him close and had him heel all the way back to their campsite.

The hike was short, and when they reached their destination, everyone set to the task of striking the camp. An easy delegation of duties commenced as they separated to do different jobs. Christoffer worked with Filip to tear down the tents and return them to their bags. With the canvases folded and stowed, they were breaking down the poles.

*"En garde,"* Christoffer saluted, twirling one of the tent's poles in one hand and waving him forward with the other.

Grinning, Filip snatched up a different pole and returned the salute. The two had a mock fight across the yard, which sent Defender barking like mad as he tried to join the fun, and had them laughing and ribbing each other to the entertainment of the others.

Deftly avoiding them, Aleks and Zaria collected the dishes and went to rinse them off in the pond, keeping a wary eye out to avoid the lurking mermaids. They did not linger and were quickly back to the group. Zaria stowed them wet into her bag.

Henrik left the campsite to take apart his traps and snares, and to ensure the firepit was thoroughly doused. Meanwhile, Geirr collected laundry from the branches above, divvying it up amongst their bags. It did not go unnoticed that he took extra time to fold his shirts and pants.

By late afternoon the group had gathered at the shoreline to watch the horizon for Bjarke's ship and Airi's return. She came first gliding along the thermals, barely having to lift a wing to keep her height or her path steady. Circling once, twice, she landed deftly on Alek's shoulder and folded her wings, brushing only the outer shell of his ear, causing him to shiver.

"I deliver message," she sang. "Bjarke come early."

"Wonderful," said Aleks. "Well done, Airi."

"Bead?" she asked.

Aleks looked to the group questioning. Catching Christoffer's gaze, he raised an eyebrow. Handing over one of the worn beads in his possession to his friend, he watched as Aleks presented it to Airi. She took the offering eagerly, but not before nuzzling his neck and nipping at his ear. Then, bead in beak, she flew off to a nearby rock where she examined and played with her prize. All the while Skorri followed her movements with a greedy gleam in his eyes.

The others continued to gaze along the horizon, but Christoffer decided to drop his bag and rest, using it as a makeshift pillow. Anticipating that most adventures have a lot of downtime between interesting events, and figuring the designation of 'early' could mean anything, he opted to catch up on sleep.

Defender disagreeing, plopped down next to him and licked his face. "Woof."

"Okay, okay, enough already," he murmured, slinging an arm around the dog and wrestling him. Defender squirmed and yipped and rolled over onto his back, presenting his belly, looking for scratches and attention.

"There's the ship," said Filip, spotting the vessel a short while later.

It dashed swiftly through the surge and foam, making headway to their location. Several yards offshore it anchored, and a tender was dropped into the water. Two figures were aboard, one clearly being the captain. It motored swiftly through the waves and pulled ashore.

Bjarke spoke first. "King Aleks, yer raven summoned me to yer side. What do ye require?"

"We are very close to winning the trust of this white raven," he said, gesturing to Skorri in the background.

"He insists he will not go with us, unless we can tell him his master's true name," said Zaria.

Bjarke cocked his head in confusion. "Why, then, need ye me?"

She held out her hands in appeal. "We must complete three challenges in order to solve three riddles before we can formulate it."

"The Lonely One is his former master," supplied Christoffer at the river-troll's confusion.

"We're down to one final challenge and we need your help to complete it," said Aleks. "You have a ship and a crew. May we borrow them?"

Bjarke's brow furrowed. "Me crew?"

"We must perform and succeed at a traditional Viking challenge," he explained. "Do you have oars?"

Bjarke's eyebrows flew up. "Me *Ursula* is a modern ship. Ye not be performing what ye seek on her. There be no oars."

Christoffer grinned at the others. "If there's no oars, does that mean there's only ands? Does this mean I get a pony *and* a suit of armor?"

"What are you talking about?" growled Bjarke, vexation darkening his brow.

"That's okay," Zaria interjected, frowning his way. Christoffer clasped his hands behind his back and pretended to whistle innocently. She shook her head fondly at him before refocusing on the troll. "I can supply the oars."

"And what about the rest of it?" asked Bjarke, scratching his rounded belly.

"Can you do the task or not?" Skorri asked, coming over to sit atop Henrik's golden antlers. The Stag Lord's sigh was full of long-suffering, causing Christoffer to snicker. The ravens really did like to roost there.

"We can," Henrik insisted, folding his arms. "Zaria can transform one of the Captain's tenders into a longship with a temporary enchantment and conjure up some oars to steer it."

"That may be, but do ye know what yer asking with a challenge like this? Who will do the deed?"

"I will," said Aleks solemnly. He looked to the others. "If it involves a ship, I am the best bet."

Henrik readily agreed, but Geirr frowned. "You don't even know what the bird is asking."

The troll gazed out across the water. "I do, though it's been an age since I've seen it done. In my youth the Vikings would set out every summer to test their agility and speed by running the oars."

"Running the oars?" pressed Aleks.

"Aye. Ye must make it round the ship while the rowers continue to row without falling into the drink. Only the nimblest of crewmen could hope to win the honors. Many tried but fewer than a quarter succeeded, even with training."

"That doesn't sound very easy," Filip said.

"It sounds amazing," said Christoffer, near to gushing. "Like a real-life video game challenge."

Geirr rolled his eyes. "You're demented. You're likely to get whacked by the oars headfirst into the ocean."

He turned to his friend. "What do you think Aleks?"

"I can run it as a fox."

"You are the best choice," said Henrik.

"But not the only choice. I am the best climber, I could do it, too."

"What does that have to do with this?"

"Everything," said Christoffer. "I have mad skills. I am like a goat."

"You are a great giddy goat," teased Zaria.

"Or Greatest Oar-jumping Athletic Teen," he boasted. "Get it? Goat."

Geirr groaned and hid his face in his hand, shaking his head. "It's not funny."

"Let me do this one, please, please," begged Christoffer. "Please, Aleks. I goat this. I swear."

"Okay, okay, no more goat puns," relented Aleks, accepting a hug from Christoffer. "I can't handle another one."

"Promise," he swore and then whooped for joy, excited to participate in a meaningful way. He jerked his shirt off, throwing it on top of his bag. Defender sniffed it curiously and then ignored it, wandering away to find something else.

"Not that I'm complaining," said Zaria, eyeing his clothing and then him, appreciatively. "But why does everyone keep taking off their shirts?"

"Not everyone," said Airi, glancing meaningfully at Aleks and Geirr.

He tossed her a cheeky wink and struck a pose. "I want to be like the cool kids."

"You goat to be kidding me," said Aleks laughingly.

"Hey I thought you said no more goat puns," pouted Christoffer.

"I said I couldn't handle another from you. I never said I wouldn't give as good as I goat."

Geirr hugged his ears. "You both should stop."

"Naaaaahhh," they bleated together, forcing a wry grin from their mocking friend.

# Chapter Fourteen: Vikings Did It

Perched on top of the rail, Christoffer clung daringly to the ropes above and beside him. He listened with half an ear as the others found their positions and went over last minute preparations. He concentrated on feeling the movement of the water and the roll of the longboat. He couldn't believe he was about to do true hero's work.

Through careful coordination between Bjarke and Aleks, they had organized the river-troll's crew into a slick rowing machine with the fairy king taking lead as coxswain on a conjured drum set at the stern. He practiced drum rolls, finding a rhythm that the crew could follow easily.

"She's a beaut' even if she's a bit irregular," hummed Bjarke from the front by the bow. "If she performs well I am inclined to keep her."

"Sure," said Zaria affably, smiling at her handiwork.

Her transfiguration of the river-troll's tender into a fully-fledged Viking vessel had been swift. The tender had melted, stretched, and reformed faster than someone could mash and sculpt a putty figurine. Approximately 21 meters long by 15 meters across, she – as Bjarke had noted – the longboat was not a traditional vessel of wood and sail.

Where one might expect wood, the ship was molded from carbon fiberglass, the material used for the tender. It cut a slick figure through the waves, rolling and surging with grace. At her figurehead was a seahorse or, perhaps, a water-wyvern. It was a bit hard to tell as only the top half of the creature was visible, and with the mouth closed Christoffer couldn't check for teeth, though he suspected it was a tribute to Vingar.

Shields of painted wood with metal trimmings decorated the hull like gemstones catching the setting sunlight. As for the sail, some ellefolken girls hoisted a cheerful cadmium yellow square canvas into place in less than two minutes, securing it fast. A white stag emblem blazed triumphantly across its center. Christoffer wondered if it had been someone's blanket, bearing tribute to Henrik.

There were thirty-two oarsmen benches, sixteen on each side, and all singly stationed. Elves and ellefolken sat on short, crate-like benches waiting and watching for their signals to start. An air of excitement floated up from the group as Bjarke explained what would happen next. They eyed Christoffer and the raven and each other, wondering how the task would go.

"Ready?" asked Henrik from his place among the oarsmen.

"As long as I don't get blisters, I'll be fine," Geirr said, from behind him. He peered longingly at Aleks' spot and gave a wistful sigh.

"He wasn't asking you," Aleks said, rolling his eyes.

"I know."

"If you knew, why did you –"

Filip grinned, ignoring them, snorting in glee when Christoffer mimed the bickering. When Aleks and Geirr turned to look, both were all innocence, which immediately earned them hard, suspicious stares. They laughed, ignoring the annoyed looks aimed at them.

Stretching his arms and shoulders, before resuming position on the oar, Filip said, "Remember, mate, to keep your focus. Don't mess up."

"You worry too much," he called out. "This'll be fun."

"That's why we worry," Filip shouted back, laughing.

"Are you ready to go?" came Bjarke's gruff voice beside him.

"Gah!" shouted Christoffer, clutching his heart. "I didn't even see you sneak up. Weren't you over there just a minute ago?"

Bjarke looked down his nose at him. "I'm going to have Aleks start them. Once Skorri gives the signal ye can start. Ye'll want us at speed, because if the timing is off ye'll end in the briny deep."

"You think he'd have me start too soon?"

Bjarke shrugged. "Why would he want ye to succeed?"

"Fair point," Christoffer replied, jumping up and down on his heels. "I'm ready."

Bjarke nodded to Aleks and the drumbeat started. At first low and steady. Rat. Tat. Tat. Slow to start, the longboat lurched jerkily as the rowers struggled to find their groove together. Swish. Swash. Swish.

As the rhythm picked up it became a roll. The drum went rat-tat-tat-tat. Rat-tat-tat-tat. Rat-tat-tat-tat. The oars swished, swished, swished. When the oarsmen stroked in time and sync, the white raven gave a trill for him to start, so at least there he was honest.

Pausing on the rail, he watched the movements of the oars weave in and out of the water, mentally picturing his path along them and around the ship. The rat-tat-tat-tat called out and the answering swish, swish, swish washed over him until he could feel them both in his body. When the oars plunged beneath the waves, his legs bent and he jumped.

The crack of the oar against his feet startled him and his muscles locked. He managed to jump again before it dipped and disappeared under the next wave, but his timing was poor. Christoffer lurched forward, windmilling and racing ahead as he staggered across two oars, missed a third, barely touched a fourth, and knocked a shin into the fifth before slipping ignominiously off the sixth and into the freezing sea.

"Ahhh!"

The longboat sailed right past him, leaving him in open water before Aleks managed to halt their momentum. He struck out towards the vessel, as Aleks reversed them and brought the ship back to him. They met not quite in the middle and an oar was stretched out. Christoffer grabbed it and they hauled him upward and back into the boat where he flopped like a fish.

"You didn't even get a quarter of the way around," remarked Geirr. "We're doomed."

"Practice run," he said, grinning and rubbing a shin. "I'll get it next time for sure."

"Try picturing the water as lava," Zaria suggested helpfully, handing him a towel to dry his hair.

"That'll light a fire under him," joked Geirr, with a wry grin, nudging Henrik who shook his head in amusement.

"That's not punny," Christoffer said, poking his tongue out.

"Actually, it is," he countered, laughing.

Christoffer threw the wet towel at him. Geirr made a face and pulled it away from his mouth and neck. With a smirk he tossed it back, but Christoffer caught it before it landed, causing his friend to pout at the failed retribution.

"Problems?" asked Aleks, waving a drumstick.

"Only that I've yet to see these mad jumps Christoffer claimed he could do," Geirr said, propping his arms against the oar.

"Oh, don't worry. I got ups. You wait and see."

Airi croaked from the mast, "Round two?"

Skorri bobbed his head in agreement. "It might stay light all night, but I still want to sleep."

"Quit your bellyaching," Aleks muttered. "You're the one that wanted these challenges."

"No," retorted Skorri. "That was your Stag Lord."

Henrik inclined his head. "It was me."

"Ready all, row," Airi said, knocking and mimicking Aleks' rhythm from before.

Following her lead, he joined in on the drum and the crew snapped to attention. Elvish men in the center of the ship began chanting, counting strokes to the beat. Soon all joined in and the longboat zipped along the surface of the sea. Christoffer took a deep breath and prepared for the first jump and subsequent impact.

On the downstroke he launched himself and with a similar crack landed on the first oar. The ellefolken woman grunted at his weight and leaned into her stroke. He leapt to the next oar, landing on one foot, and took to running.

Timing nearly perfect, he only stumbled when reaching the oars in the back. His transition into the boat, over to the opposite side, and onto the second half lacked finesse, and he slipped. Foot sliding one way, he slid the other and in an unmanly superman dive ran chest first into the next oar, crashing unceremoniously into the water. There was no recovery.

Sinking under the waves, he felt paralyzed, the wind knocked out of him. Clutching his chest, he kicked for the surface and treaded water to keep afloat. When his lungs released their hold on him, he sucked in great gulps of air, wheezing and choking. The shadow of the longboat fell over him and he gratefully accepted help to reach the deck.

"Ow," he complained in everyone's presence, thankful for Zaria's fresh towel.

At the back of the boat, Aleks spoke with the rowers nearest him. "Don't think of it as a circular motion. It's more elliptical. In sweep-out sweep-pause-in sweep again."

Zaria, who'd been listening brightened. "Oh like a *rond de jambe en l'air.*"

"A Rhonda samba lair – what?" asked one of the women, hesitating mid stroke.

She shook her hand. "Sorry. Ignore me. Ballet."

"Bah lay?" the woman asked more confused.

"Never mind," Zaria said. "Forget I said anything."

"We should knot the string around the oar locks tighter," Filip said, fingering the loose twist of twine at his station.

"Good idea," agreed Aleks. "Everyone take a minute to do that."

Skorri shook his wings out and refolded them. "Won't matter. He'll still fail, and you'll all lose."

"We're not pessimistic like you," Zaria said, wrapping Christoffer in a loose hug, steadily meeting the raven's mocking gaze. "We have faith in our friend."

"We do?" teased Geirr. She shot him a quelling look and he raised his hands in surrender. "We do."

When everything was reset, Christoffer climbed the railing for the third and final attempt. This time he knew he'd succeed and not just because he had to in order to win. His perspective was different and he felt equally a sense of hyper awareness and of separation. Instead of sinking into the beat of the drums, he stayed above it. The feeling, a cross between being in the zone, laser focused for the task ahead, and strangely, like watching oneself from a distance, out of body.

He felt more like a character from one of his games in the midst of great test of skill than like himself. He was the hero of the moment, if not of the story. Rat-tat-tat-tat. Rat. Tat. Tat. Tat. Like a bubble dispersing, sounds crystallized and sharpened. He came back to the scene the participant instead of the witness. Alight with the anticipation of victory, he jumped.

"Don't screw up," Skorri twittered.

"Blockhead," Airi croaked, fluttering to the other side of the mast.

Jarred and distracted, his saving grace on the first half of the run lay solely in his previous two attempts. His feet, well aware of the dangers, piloted him forward until he regained his footing and his sense of balance. Hopping from one oar shaft to the next, he quickly made it to the end of the first half and stumbled into the boat. Hands on knees, he caught his breath.

"Easy," Aleks called and the rowing slowed. He held his hand up in preparation to give the stop command.

Skorri, however, nibbled on his foot unconcerned. He said, disinterestedly and with an air of superiority, "You've got another half to do."

Christoffer gestured to the new half. "I know, I know. Only this time I'm running opposite of the way they're rowing. I need a minute. I only get one chance."

"One minute," the raven reluctantly allowed.

"Or more," wheedled Christoffer, straightening and going to the opposite rail. After a few more deep breaths he nodded to Aleks at the bow.

"In two, high ten," the fairy king called.

Aleks and the oarsmen picked up speed. The drum rolled and tapped. Ten strokes later he called for the crew to settle. The oars continued to sluice silkily through the waves, but at a slower rate than the ones used to gain speed.

Christoffer watched as the blades stroked through the water, catching at the same time. He noted who seemed to be lagging behind the others, unable to drive the stroke as quickly. His friend saw the same and called out seats to fall in and fall out as needed. Three strokes later they all rowed together evenly.

He readied his stance on the rail and launched himself forward, meeting the strokes. Pinwheeling forward, he ran the oars as fast as he could. They rapidly disappeared under his feet like a sinking island. Halfway there Christoffer knew he was going to fail. He couldn't keep up the pace.

As coxswain Aleks saw it, too. "On the square."

The crew stopped feathering their strokes, making it easier for Christoffer to land his jumps. Three oars passed quickly. He might just have a shot at passing this challenge.

Airi hopped up and down agitatedly. "Take the run off. Take the run off."

"No," shouted Aleks, but it was too late, the rowers placed their oars at angles into the water, and stopped rowing.

Christoffer used the lack of strokes to throw himself forward. Three more done and two left. He leapt and flung his arms out, catching his weight against the side of the boat. It lurched drunkenly under him, causing those on the opposite side of the boat to shout in alarm. At least one splash was heard.

Hands grabbed at his forearms and hauled him upright and into the boat. Laughter rang out as two elves were brought in soaking wet on the other side. They grinned sheepishly to everyone and waved. Christoffer clapped the shoulders of those elves and ellefolken on his left and right and grinned. He'd done it. He'd done it. He'd actually done it!

Skorri raised his tail feathers and let out a poop. It landed with a wet plop on the deck below. He croaked, "You cheated."

Affronted, Christoffer straightened up and crossed his arms. "Did not."

"The crew stopped rowing. It doesn't count."

"It certainly does," said Henrik, abandoning his seat.

Christoffer nodded forcefully. "I ran the oars like you asked. I finished both sides without falling into the water."

The white raven scoffed. "Does not. They helped you get back into the boat. You forfeit."

"Are you offering us a chance for a redo?" Zaria asked.

"Zaria!" Christoffer shouted, aghast. At the same time, Skorri shrieked nervously, "No redos!"

"Then you can't say we didn't complete the challenge," she reasoned.

"That's not how it works," grumbled Skorri, glaring at her from his perch.

"We still need to figure out the riddles," she added. "We only have a single guess left. What's the harm?"

"You might get it," he said.

"We might not."

He thought about it and bobbed his head reluctantly. "One guess. Then your spell."

Christoffer whooped and scooped her up in a hug. "Guys, did you see that? I did it. That was awesome!"

Filip pried Zaria away and wrestled him, locking him in a hold and scrubbing his head. He pushed the blond off, fixing his hair into a less messy do.

"Where were we?" asked Filip. "Can anyone remember all the clues?"

Christoffer shook his head. "It doesn't matter. We've solved one, possibly two of the riddles. We need to focus on the third."

"We can't meta this!" Aleks protested.

He gave him a bemused stare. "Can't we? What's the last clue? Wasn't it something like 'what is first and last' on this trial? What did I do first and last?"

Zaria pursed her lips. "Jump?"

He waved it away. "No that can't be it. Dayarjump makes zero sense."

"It's not Dayar," Geirr said dryly. "Why do you keep pushing that?"

He shrugged. "We haven't found anything better."

"What are ye six doing now?" asked Bjarke. "We need to return to the ship."

"We're trying to guess his previous master's name," said Aleks, pointing to Skorri.

"Harrumph. Well, I be commanding me crew again. One last time everyone. Oars at the ready."

There were a few grumbles, but the crew reseated themselves and got into position. Bjarke turned the longboat and set the course for his *Ursula* in the distance, returning them to where they started... which gave Christoffer an idea.

"In!"

"Inn? We're not going to an inn," said Henrik.

"No, no. In. As in that is the first and last thing I did. I started in the boat. I ended in the boat. In. Skorri didn't like that I'd had help into the boat. It has to be in because it certainly can't be boat or ship, just like Dayarjump, Dayarboat and Dayarship is out. In. I'm sure of it. It's short and sweet and could append to someone's name."

"In? Like Day-ar-in? Darrin?" asked Zaria.

"Yes," said Christoffer.

"Is that your final guess?" questioned Skorri eagerly.

Christoffer wagged a finger at him. "Not yet it isn't." He turned to the others. "He's too willing to accept that answer. It's not it."

"Or it's what he wants us to think," said Filip. "Wait. Are we sure it's not oar? You ran the oars. First and last thing you touched."

"He's not that smart," said Christoffer confidently.

"Are you sure, mate? He seems pretty smart."

"But not as sharp as a fox. What do you think Aleks?"

"Dayaroar isn't half bad, but no it can't be that and I'm with Christoffer on this – it can't be Darrin either."

"Do we try the other syllable?" asked Zaria. "What about Day-er-in? Day-er-oar?"

"Is that –"

They turned as one on the bird. "No!"

He shrunk back and glared at them with venom. "You tell me when it is, then."

Filip ticked them off on his fingers, "D for dagaz."

"Er," added Henrik.

"In," Christoffer said, firmly, eliminating oar.

"D."

"Er."

"In."

Zaria mouthed it out twice more before looking at them. "Dee-er-in? That's doesn't roll off the tongue at all. It sounds like mumbo-jumbo."

"Are we sure it's three syllables and not two?" Aleks asked.

"Like Deer-in?" guessed Geirr.

"What if we change which syllable to emphasize? See how the name changes when I focused more on the 'er' and less on the D," said Christoffer, thinking back to the raven's earlier slip of the tongue. "Instead of Deer-in what about Dur-in?"

"Wait, yer not talking about Durrin inn Kyrri are ye?" asked Bjarke, having overheard, and earning an outraged squawk from the raven. "I thought he moved in with cousins in Finland. When did he get back? Are ye saying he's the Lonely One? I didn't know he owned a raven. He still owes me for his last passage inland. Who's going to pay that?"

"That's our final guess," said Christoffer elatedly, triumph in his breast.

"You ruined everything," cried Skorri, stamping a foot and knocking agitatedly.

# Epilogue: Escort Mission Unlocked

"Way enough," called Bjarke and the crew stopped rowing.

The longboat glided alongside *Ursula* and was quickly secured to the ship's side. Ellefolken and elves scurried up the ladder returning to their positions. Christoffer and his friends followed suit, climbing the side of the sailing vessel. Bjarke joined them on deck.

"We must fetch Olaf next and return to shore. Where will I be dropping ye off?"

Henrik conferred with Aleks on the best spot and relayed it to the captain. The river-troll grunted and headed off to talk with his second in command. The others ambled to the mess for victuals and cider. Defender followed his nose after them.

Geirr hesitated and backtracked, joining him at the rail. They lingered in the twilight companionably, watching as the sun kissed the sea and held there, bobbing on the edge like a floating beach ball, orange and red and fiery. Clouds scuttled pleasantly across the sky, casting shadows on the water.

Taking a deep breath of the salty air, Christoffer smiled, pleased with his accomplishment. He'd done what he set out to do and proved he was integral to the success of the quest. He was proud of himself.

"Not bad for us ordinary humans, huh?" he said, bumping shoulders with his quiet friend.

"There's nothing ordinary about you," Geirr teased.

"True. Or you," Christoffer said happily.

Durrin's raven alighted on the rail on his left and tucked in his wings. One steely gray-blue eye glared at him beadily. "I blame you."

"Do you?" asked Christoffer, surprised. It was Bjarke, after all, who'd given away the final answer. "Well, that's fine, I guess. I can take it."

Geirr leaned around him to stare at the bird. "Cheer up; you and Master Brown have a lot in common."

The raven made a raspberry sound. "Whatever happens next is your fault."

"Oh, quit being such a grouch," Geirr said. "You need this as much as we do."

"Do not," Skorri pouted.

"Do too."

"Whatever. Just be sure to escort me there safely. I want to make a good impression."

"That's a first," Geirr said under his breath.

Christoffer laughed at their bickering. He turned to the raven. "Escort missions are great side quests."

"What is he talking about, now?" the raven grumped, looking to Geirr for clues.

"Beats me," he said.

"We have our overall goal, right? This is just another mission in a series of smaller tasks designed to get us there. How many does that make up to this point?"

"I don't know," said Geirr, raising an eyebrow.

"You're not making any sense to me," Skorri sneered.

"At least four or five by my count," Christoffer said, ticking them off on his fingers. "First there was the troll's information gathering mission; next, came the queen's quest; then, the witch's checkpoint; after that, the raven's challenge; and now we have the escort mission." Something shimmered under the water, catching his attention. Whale? Dolphin? Winter-wyvern? He pointed. "Do you see that?"

Geirr angled his head and peered down. "What? I don't see anything."

Christoffer looked again and found the water returned to normal. He blinked his eyes and stared harder. Waves rolled languidly below him. "I could have sworn there was a shadow moving."

"Probably just the ship's," said Geirr.

He frowned. The sun was at the wrong angle for that, but... then what could it have been? After nothing further happened he shook his head and turned to his friend. "I must have imagined it."

"All right, then. Let's eat. What do you say? You hungry, oh man of the hour?"

"Does a bear poop in the woods?"

Geirr pulled a face. "I swear you get cornier every time you open your mouth. Did you just say poop?"

"You love me," Christoffer said, walking toward the door where their friends disappeared below deck.

"That's debatable," said Geirr, rolling his eyes.

"You can say that again," groused Skorri.

"That's debatable."

"Everyone's a comedian," he whined. "Shouldn't I have the last joke?"

Geirr shoved him through and down the steps. "Sure, sure. Don't get your goat up."

"You did it again. No fair!"

# Thanks for Reading

I hope you enjoyed the beginning of Christoffer's trilogy. If you could take two minutes to write a review on your favorite bookseller's website, it would be greatly appreciated. Your reviews help other readers discover the enchanting world of Norway, Zaria Fierce, Aleks Mickelsen, Christoffer Johansen, and their friends and make all the difference in the world. A good story is best shared and in doing so you would absolutely make my day.

## An Invitation

Stay in touch! You can subscribe to my free author newsletter at my website. If you do, you'll get a free copy of book two in the series, learn about upcoming releases, get behind the scenes information, and more. As a bonus, I've created desktop backgrounds using some of Eoghan's artwork from earlier in the Zaria Fierce series, which you'll also get for free when you sign up. https://keiragillett.com/free-download/

# The Adventure Continues:

## Christoffer Johansen and the Gyllenhammar of Malmdor

Get a sneak peek of the next book in the Zaria Fierce world, featuring Christoffer's adventures:

https://keiragillett.com/book/gyllenhammar/

# About the Author and Artist:
# Keira Gillett

Every chance she can, Keira Gillett loves to take ballet lessons, where she calls fondus nasty one-legged squats, and grande battements the reason you happily suffer barre routines featuring said fondus. At home, she loves to play with her doggie and train him to learn new tricks. Spin is the closest he gets to a pirouette. Wherever he goes, even without a tutu Oskar steals all the attention, not unlike Christoffer. You can follow Keira and Oskar's antics on Instagram with the #oskarpie hashtag.

Find Keira at https://keiragillett.com/

# About the Artist: Kaitlin Statz

Kaitlin Statz grew up in many different places, but currently lives in Sarasota, FL with her partner, Travis, and their young dog, Eezo. She attended New College of Florida and the University of Oxford for a life in the sciences before returning to her true love, art. She started her work as Statz Ink in 2015 and has been creating art ever since.

Find her at http://www.statzink.com/